Home Grown

Grown

WELCOME TO J-POD

Tressa Rich
COOL CHICK CHRONICLES

Table of Contents

January 3, 2007 4

Love Letter 1 13

Happy New Year! Finally, this year! 16

The Farm: The Calm Before 22

The Raid 28

The Search is On! 41

The Ride of Your Life 50

The CCADC: More In-take 60

Brian and Diana... 69

The Bleeding Hearts Club Band...................... 80

Nightmare on Cherokee Street........................ 87

Girl Interrupted: Morning Comes 96

No Talking! 110

Another 18 Hours 115

Welcome to J-Pod! 119

T.G.I.F.! 132

Life Lines 143

J-Pod: Lunch	151
Frank, Dee and Fam to the Rescue	156
No Panties! No Bra! And No Socks for You!	164
Do you want bread with that?	173
Low Life Saga	181
Does "dumb" hold up in Court?	195
The Net is Cast	205
Letters: Tess, Mom and Evan	212

January 3, 2007
As she sat at her computer diligently typing an email, movement outside the large double window caused Tess to glance up from the screen. In the beautiful, lush pasture, framed by majestic old oaks that had to be a few hundred years old predating the Civil War, a luminescent, dappled grey Arabian horse came prancing and snorting by, tail held up, neck arched, nostrils flaring.

A funny feeling rose in her chest as it swelled with pride and love. It absolutely took her breath away. She stood up for a better vantage point in time to see the grey mare's foal, now just six months, galloping as fast as it could, down the slightly sloping terrain, her delicate body leaning in like a motorcycle making a turn. The mother horse stopped abruptly, striking a pose, as still as a statue, erect, ears pricked forward, intently looking into the distance.

Tess sighed and smiled as she took in the view. The four-board black stained fencing drew out the boundary lines of her small suburban horse farm tucked neatly into the foothills of the North Georgia Mountains. Just two years before, she would have never guessed she would be here, with horses, selling real estate, working from home in her dream job! And with her dream man too! She was on top of the world and felt truly blessed. She took a deep breath, closed her eyes and felt it.

When Tess and Evan eventually got together, it was a whirlwind romance...the kind you read about. It was a delayed start when their paths first crossed at a concert, where neither were with a date. They talked a little bit, exchanged numbers, but then he never called. They were both in relationships that were coming to a close. The timing just wasn't right. But there was something about Evan that stuck in her mind. Tess remembered his engaging green eyes, warm smile and restless black curls that framed a handsome and kind face.

After that fateful meeting, Tess's thoughts would turn to him at random. Usually at night as she lay in her bed, naked and alone. She even had a vivid dream about him that left her breathless and even more curious. She went on with her life, trying not to obsess about him, but it was hard not to. It had been so long since she had been interested in anyone. She was lonely. He was so sweet and charming and handsome.

Tess was now "pushing 40." She couldn't believe it! 38 had come quickly. In the blink of an eye. She was ready for a serious relationship, having pushed that aside all these years as she pursued her career path and lived a nice life with her Mom BFF as her roommate since her step-father had passed 7 years prior.

"He would have called if he was interested..." she lamented, but she was too busy to worry about it (too much).

And busy she was! As a marketing manager at a real estate brokerage with Top Bitch of East Cobb Deborah Radford. Little did she know what she was in for after making the transition from a lay-off as an account executive from one of the big ad agencies in Atlanta. Sure, the real estate work was totally cookie-cutter, writing copy for ads for houses, marketing positionings for the various agents that would come and go, flyers, layouts... compared to the multi-million dollar accounts and businesses she had been exposed to over the last 15 years. Tess had been an integral part of strategic and creative teams in her past, worked major campaigns and events, supported several dynamic CEOs. This was child's play in comparison.

Her role at the mom and pop real estate office was "ok." She had to take the job and take the passive aggressive treatment from Debbie. She was thankful to have a job, even at a fraction of what she had been making. After 9/11 happened, it was rough for a lot of people. And she found that she really loved real estate. It was putting up with the backstabbing and passive aggressive vibes of the insecure Broker she was wary of. But, she had to take the job. And had to take it from Radford and smile.

Tess bought and sold her own homes over the years and sold up each time. She had been lucky, but was also a little savvy. Her marketing sense and style didn't hurt either. She didn't miss the hellish commute in Atlanta's worse-than-LA traffic, or rallying for position within the Agency, traveling to events and meetings at the drop of a hat, pulling all-nighters getting ready for pitches, no matter how exciting it was. She was ready to settle down now and slow down too. But, things had just happened a little out of sequence and a little too soon for her plan. When Broker Bitch Deborah terminated her abruptly (she really didn't know what for), without cause, and after a positive review, she went ahead and got her real estate license.

Tess was a survivor...even with her bruised ego ... feeling like she had been shunned by the advertising industry she had poured her heart and soul into for almost two decades, overlooked, discarded...it was time to move on. Concede like many do who get into real estate. She could put on her other alter-ego and do this, even though it wasn't really her. Putting herself out there as a real estate agent wasn't the plan, but she did think she could do something in real estate. Some investments. Foreclosure flips maybe?

Tess was an exotically beautiful brunette who didn't know how pretty she was. She learned since her teens to dress down and not be sexy, having come up in a military town where drawing attention to yourself at all was trouble. She had a good head on her shoulders, and was a good girl with a heart of gold. She was really the whole package. Maybe that was the problem. She often thought maybe if she was more frivolous, more flirtatious possibly, that could have helped her career. Was blowing off advances from a client or even other account managers what hurt her career advancement? She sometimes wondered. She just wasn't that type of person.

She was a true sweetheart and a hard worker. Since she was 16, she worked. Worked her way through school. Bought her first home when she was 24. Sold up from there and bought a foreclosure, which she flipped a few years later and made a cool $50k. Not too bad. So, it was a natural transition to get into real estate, even though that was the furthest thing from her mind when she was starting out to make her mark in the business and entertainment world in HotLanta.

When Tess first got her real estate license, she thought she would just buy and sell her own properties. She didn't know what she wanted to do, but had to do something! She couldn't imagine her face out there with a slogan "Tess is the best for your real estate needs!" Her stomach churned at the thought. But as fate would have it, she ended up incorporating her rekindled passion for horses with selling estate horse farms and working with the elite horsey-set in Alpharetta. Tess landed with top broker Bob Nardelli in the high-end and celebrity dotted equestrian area. She let her horse sense and marketing prowess take the lead. In less than two years she was on the verge of really making it in this very competitive and select market. She talked the talk and walked the walk and followed Bob's lead.

Tess and Evan reconnected later that year and things went really fast. Both in their late 30s, it was a second chance at love. Evan was the epitome of Tess's ideal man...sexy, kind, sensitive, spiritual, strong family values, entrepreneurial, smart, fun. And, the fact that he thought she was a Goddess didn't hurt matters. He talked open-heartedly and sincerely and told her early-on that she was "the one." Her heart soared!

For Evan, the first few years of the relationship were spent tying up loose ends, trying to solidify his career, being the "man" of several families including for his Mother, Sister and Niece, and for his Son who was about to graduate high school and ex- wife. He took his honor to the extreme and went above and beyond as far as family duty was concerned. Tess patiently waited her turn.

Evan encouraged Tess with her real estate endeavors. He had a few rental houses of his own, worked with remodeling and had a passion for real estate that rivaled her own. Evan had grown up helping his Dad who was a real estate broker and appraiser in the 1980s. So, he was no stranger to the business. He worked with several commercial clients he knew from being in the automotive trade and was called to assist in zoning matters, once more building the family name with different county commissioners. He and Tess were a good team.

The couple was not only in alignment with their feelings for each other, but also their views on wanting to make real estate investments that could yield a higher return than what was left of Tess's 401k. She definitely wanted to reinvest her money in real estate as all the mutual funds in her portfolio had been slipping steadily downward since the 9/11 tragedy.

They dove head first in love and life together. With Tess's good credit and Evan's good contacts, they didn't look back. Now, putting it all on the line to have her dream farm and dream man, she had all she could have asked for...a beautiful property with her dogs and horses, her own thriving real estate business, a great life partner. Life was good. Little did she know it was all about to change.

Love Letter 1

Dear Love,
It is so good to hear from you. Don't worry about venting in some of your letters. I want to hear it all. I am with you in all of it...the good, bad, happy, sad. All of it. Always! I belong with you!!!!

I know it's tough being apart. Being here, away from you, is hard, but it is so much better than never having you. Even on my worst day here, it is better than my best day with any else before you came into my life. I know I tell you that often. It is because it is what is truly in my heart.

I also tell you that hearing from or thinking about anyone else always makes me really appreciate you and love you even more. That's not a line. It is how I have always felt about you since Blue Ridge.

I have told you these things in the best of times and now in the worst of times. I have also said them in many times in between. It is because I always feel that way. It is at the core of my being. In all the years we have been together have I ever paid or shown you anything different than that?

Rather than be upset with what I don't have, I try to appreciate and be thankful for all the things I do have. I treasure our relationship. I am so thankful for our family and our good health. We have already come through so much together and have each grown.

I have thoughts many times about the mistakes I made that caused you to get in trouble also. I am very sorry to put you though that first month but in my heart of hearts I can't wish for it be any different.

I hope that the strength, understanding and appreciation of things you have gained from this experience along with the closeness and understanding of each other we will each have, is worth to you the price you paid for it.

It had to happen this way for us to grow. I know you understand because I can feel it.

My orendi is very high now and I am able to do even more than I ever have all of the time you have known me. I have asked for and been given protection and resources for you while I am here. The money will come. You will not have to bankrupt or be without any necessity. Look up, not down. It all comes from God, not us. I have been allowed to ask for and you have been allowed to receive because we are in alignment with God's will.
Claim it. It is already yours.
I love you!
Evan

Happy New Year! Finally, this year!
Just a few days into the New Year she had such hopes and optimism. Finally, it would be the year they were going to get ahead, pay off the enormous debts incurred on behalf of a few money-pit investment properties/fixer uppers and be poised to take over the high-end North Fulton Alpharetta real estate market. This was to be the year Tess' business would soar. Evan's big zoning case and commission was expected to come through. All their debts would be paid. They could add to their portfolio of properties with a weekend cabin at Lake Arrowwood. Maybe Tess could get pregnant! They would definitely get married. This year...

Evan said often that he wished he would have proposed on their first date. He knew then, but didn't want to scare her away. They had worked through most of their issues personally and as a couple now. This was going to be their year. Evan could feel it he said.

He had a lot on his plate...several rental houses, another they were trying to finish and put on the market, requests from his mother, from his business associates and subs, plus his son starting college.

Evan had a busy day planned, as most of his were, since his son had started in his freshman year at KSU. He and Tess had little time together...this whole last year, with only fleeting moments of enjoyment together on their newly acquired mini-farm. What a beautiful place it was! Nothing fancy, but the land, the rolling hills, lush pastures, big old oak trees and the vibe of the place was just right.

"For the first time in my life I feel at home and don't want for anyone else or anything," Evan would often revel, "I'm truly blessed to be here and with 'the one.'"

Tess agreed and knew that the leap of faith she had taken leveraging her good credit a little over a year ago to get this place had been worth it. "If they'll loan me ½ a million to buy this place, we'll figure out a way to pay for it!" she declared. And, her real estate sales had been there one right after the other and Evan's projects were soon to be paying off too. They were on a roll.

Spring and Summer passed with two foals being born, blooms were popping up all over the farm. Wonderful surprises of color splashing at random. The sparkling pool adjacent to the stables, looked over a grassed riding arena and provided welcome respite to the summer heat and humidity that has you dripping and your clothes sticking to you by noon.

After doing her barn work and caring for the horses and dogs, Tess would often take a quick look to make sure no one was around, peel off her sticky, damp and dusty barn clothes for a refreshing skinny dip in the softness of the salt water pool. It was a dream floating there looking up into the picture powder blue sky, a hawk effortlessly gliding above way up high.

Pure heaven. Then with a big splash, here comes Mac, a Dalmatian, her big baby boy rescue dog...who thought he was a Lab. After some swimming, barn chores and horse feeding done, she heads into the rustic ranch house currently still in the process of being renovated...to her office to get to work...answering emails and doing property searches. Those were the days of Summer...now a distant memory.

Christmas and New Year's just past, it was time to get back into the saddle and get back to work. Two of Tess's deals had fallen through over the last several months and was a big loss of almost $25,000 in commissions. Her Broker was encouraging and supportive, but she was still concerned. Feast or famine...that's what they say about the real estate business.

Evan had been supportive and told her he was now ready to get behind her business more and help out as much as he could. Tess had also just completed the courses to get her Broker's license and was going to schedule her State exam as soon as she could get the extra money for it.

"I sure hope so. I am worried sick." she let him know. "How are you going to come up with so much money. I can get the last that I have from my 401k, but then that's it." Tess was anguished. She told Evan before she closed the deal on the farm that she couldn't (and wouldn't) swing it without his support of at least half the expenses. Now with her lack of income for months and his inconsistent cash flow, she didn't know what they were going to do. More than anything else, she wanted to keep the farm. So did Evan.

"You just focus on your real estate. Get some sales on the books!" he tried to encourage her. She held on to his strong chest and buried her head. And with a kiss on the forehead and another squeeze, he was off!

She was sad, worried and tired of this stress. She trusted him, but was wary.

The last several years she'd been waiting, waiting, waiting! ...waiting for a ring, waiting for the debts to start getting paid back, waiting for the houses to get finished and ready for sale, waiting for Evan to tie up his loose ends and focus on their relationship, waiting for him to finally focus on her!

He did have other obligations which she had accepted and she knew he loved her dearly...but it was all wearing thin.

"I know it's been a tough road, but I'm not going anywhere. We're a team." he pleaded. "I want to be married and to have a family and to do all that we've talked about. I want to be home more and I'm ready for us to be able to spend time together. I'm tired of working 24/7. It won't be like this much longer." he reassured her. "I want to be here on the farm with you and have a life." His cell phone rang and he pushed away, telling the caller he was on his way.

"Love you." she uttered, standing there with stall pick in hand in the middle of the aisle of the empty barn, the dust from the gravel drive bustling up from the truck tires as he took off down the drive.

The Farm: The Calm Before
It had been a productive day. The phone had been ringing and emails popping. Last year this time, the week after New Year's, had been busy and the first quarter was the best Tess had had in her two year real estate career. Her Broker Bob also had a great quarter then and between the two had sold well over $6 million. Now there was a lull. "Things have to pick up," Bob told her. "I'm ready for the New Year!"

"Me too! I've got a lot of prospects percolating. A fellow from Florida emailed me today about a $4.5 million estate on Birmingham. Five Star Ranch. I'm VERY excited about that one!" Tess chirped, happy and optimistic.

"That's a good one! Keep working it." Bob encouraged bulging out of his Pink Polo, tanned and puffed up.

Her chores were done for the evening, horses were fed, blanketed and tucked in their stalls for the night. The pine shavings ruffled as the horses shuffled about. The barn was battened down for warmth, the top stall doors latched, horses contently munching tasty Timothy hay.

It was going to be a cold one. Even in the South, January temperatures can get below freezing. Tonight was going to be in the upper 20s. As Tess came in from the barn, she thought of a nice hot bath. Even though it was only 6:00 p.m., it was already dark. Really dark out in the country with no streetlights. All was still, quiet and COLD.

Frank and DeeDee, a gregarious couple, had come to stay on the farm over the summer as caretakers and extra help with the renovations. That fateful night the pair were on their way home from the grocery store and running a few errands. They were really a hoot and helped out a lot with the work on the farm that Tess and Evan didn't calculate in addition to their daily jobs and routines.

The first of what would become surrogates to Tess on the farm, designated and selected by Evan, to be there while he couldn't, as he wheeled and dealed his way around town.

DeeDee, a "certified horticulturalist," was certainly in her element on the grounds and could name every plant, shrub, herb or tree there was. A true Southern Belle, she always ended her sentences with "Sugar, Sweetie, Hun, or ya'll" and had a course laugh and smile for everyone, snaggle teeth and all! In her overalls, tye-died t-shirt and straw hat, she flew around the yard on the riding mower, headphones on, cigarette dangling from one corner of her mouth. Total hippie-fied.

Just like the way she kept the lawn and gardens on the farm, you could tell Dee's touch in the house. Everything was always neat, organized and somehow better after she put her touch on it. She was kind, sometimes boisterous, always jovial with a "How the heck are ya!" and a sunny disposition that matched her golden hair and rosy cheeks.

Her better half, Frank, was a Slim Jim of a man. He still had his boyish good looks and glint in his eye. A handyman extra-ordinaire, Frank and DeeDee had become acquainted with Evan when a subcontractor on a job for one of his rental houses that was being prepped for sale brought them on board. Between jobs and between homes, the couple settled into the rental house sheetrocking, painting, cleaning and landscaping. When the job was done and the house sold, they had no where to go. So, in true to form, Evan invited them to come out to the farm to help out. The trial period never ended and they soon called the farm "home" and Frank the Kubota tractor his!

Tess often felt like she had a more intimate relationship with Frank and DeeDee than Evan himself who was more absent than present lately, called away more than being home. Frank became her go to guy for any "Honey-Do" items. Always cheerful and with a can-do attitude, Frank put his own sweat equity into the place, as did DeeDee.

With DeeDee, Tess capitalized on her knack with people and computer skills, grooming her to help with her real estate clients. DeeDee gave good phone and she seemed to really enjoy it.

Albeit a somewhat different arrangement, almost commune-like, it worked and everybody was happy working for the common good and the farm. They even liked the horses and shoveled manure as part of the job description...as needed, of course. That was Tess's domain.

Her beauties...the beautiful horses she hand picked to be her breeding stock of champion Arabian bloodlines. "Walk in Beauty Farm" was the name Tess and Evan had agreed on for their farm name. Based on the spiritual Native American Prayer which ends in "Walk in Beauty my friends."

Tess tried to call Evan several times late that afternoon, wondering if he'd be home in time for dinner. It was strange and worrisome that he had not answered her multiple calls. So unlike him. The cell phone was their lifeline during the day and on his travels...their connection. They spoke often, just checking in and giving updates on their day.

She felt put off and dejected, then worried as hours passed and no return call. "He's just busy." she thought. "...working, can't answer...he'll call back soon." She couldn't help but think something was wrong, but dismissed the thought and made excuses like his ringer was off, phone was dead, no charger available...something like that.

Tess distracted herself with the evening news and most importantly, the weather. She sat at the end of her bed looking up at the TV on the highboy dresser, next to the big bay window overlooking the front pasture, now just a big black window into the evening night. Her dogs sat around her feet and one on the bed beside. Such loyal companions. She was their alpha and whole world.

In the distance out front she saw headlights coming up the winding gravel drive, her automatic thought that it must be Frank and Dee returning from their errands. She returned to watching the weather. "Going to be chilly tonight, in the 30s in Atlanta and high 20s in North Georgia." the announcer reported.

"Glad the horses are in. And glad you guys are all here, safe and sound tonight!" she told her dogs, clapping her hands, the dogs getting up and rallying around her for attention. Tess laughed and smiled. Mac tried to get in her lap. He was too big for that but she let him anyway. She hugged and kissed him, he happily licked her cheek.

The Raid

The sounds of the rustic ranch house were familiar, and the squeak of the back door opening was something she had heard twenty times a day. Boots clomping on the hardwood flooring were also common. But the gruff voice calling her name, "Tess Sanderson! Tess Sanderson!" made her stand up abruptly in fear.

She turned quickly to face her bedroom door and before she could take two steps forward, two strange men in dark clothing were moving towards her. A flash of horror of a home invasion sparked in her mind. Her female dog barked but shied back, while Mac wagged his tail and looked at them like new playmates.

"I'm Tess Sanderson," she stammered. "What? Whaaaaa..." Her heart was beating wildly. She couldn't speak.

"We are Detective Broward and Detective Johnson from the Georgia Bureau of Investigation and we need to speak with you." one of the men announced.

She took a breath. Quieted her now very excited dogs and tried to maintain her composure as she calmly and cautiously tried to usher the men back into the foyer and center of the house.

The dogs circled the men, the female still on guard, barking but taking cover behind Tess. Mac jumped and wanted to play, happy to see two new prospects.

"Mac, down!" Tess commanded to deaf ears. "Dalmatians aren't deaf, they just have selective hearing." she joked to the stone faced authorities who were not amused.

"Miss Sanderson, we have Evan in custody and we need to speak with you." One of the agents declared. They looked like outdoorsmen, hunters with their dark jackets, gloves and boots. Plain clothed, good old boys with beards. One looked familiar.

"Is Evan ok?" she asked, very concerned and downright scared.

"He's fine, but we've got your dually truck and horse trailer. You need to tell us what you know about this grow house of his and you need to do it now!" the taller agent growled. "What?" she cried, still confused, just as Frank and DeeDee came in.

The dog barks came again like rapid fire. Tess tried to contain them. Frank and DeeDee took one look around at the two men and Tess standing there and their jaws dropped, and they looked like two deer caught in the headlights of a speeding Semi.

"What in the hell is going on here?" Dee bellowed.

"These men are GBI agents and they have Evan!" Tess cried. "Something's wrong. I don't know what is happening. They just got here and came in and I..." The dogs continued to bark and the situation was escalating now.

"Ok, ok everybody. Keep your hands where we can see them." One of the men instructed. The two split up with one heading to Frank and DeeDee and the other staying with Tess.

"Let me get the dogs up." Tess said and grabbed collars to put the two in the bedroom closing the door.

"Are there any weapons on the premises?" the Agent demanded.

"No, there are not." Tess answered cautiously.

"Do you have a search warrant? Are we under arrest?" she asked, obviously confused. The agents spoke between themselves retreating to a corner of the vaulted center room, still under construction. Another of Evan's unfinished home projects.

"You take them over there and I'll get her." The taller agent, Broward giving the directive and taking Tess' arm leading her over to the kitchen table at the far side of the expansive space. While Johnson stood questioning Frank and Dee, who still stood with grocery bags and keys in hand, coats on.

"Have a seat Miss Sanderson." Agent Broward ordered. His eyes were steeley and she could almost see his serpent's tongue lapping the air.

"Evan Cayce is in a whole lot of trouble. We found him in your vehicle and we've got your truck and horse trailer too. What do you know about the house on Lake Hills Drive?"

She sat abruptly down at the oak kitchen table, the overhead like like a spot light on her face for an interrogation. She got a better look at Broward and recognized him immediately.

"You're the fellow who was out here the other week scouting locations for cell phone towers." She remembered getting a flashback of the event, vividly recalling his schpeel and pitch stating how he was sourcing locations, high ground for a cell phone tower company and they would pay up to $2000 per month lease for a good location.

He had also gone to her neighbors that same day and there had been discussing if they should consider it at all.

Evan showed him around the whole property proudly. $2000 a month was a good sum, but Tess and Evan agreed they didn't want such an eyesore to take away from their beautiful pasture.

OMG she thought! "It was all a sting operation?" Evan had given this fellow a tour. Showed him all around while Tess went back to her office and back to work. Little did they know who he really was! Scoping them out and the farm.

Broward chuckled and said proudly, "Well, I wasn't being very truthful with you then…" Smug and pretty full of himself. "Now, Miss Sanderson. This can go one of two ways. We're talking houses, horses, cars…you need to cooperate with us and let us know all that you know about Evan's grow…"

"His what!" Taylor exclaimed, now getting more upset and frightened. "I don't know what you are talking about!" and she really didn't. This was all news to her.

"The grow house he has going on Lake Hills drive. We found over 300 plants there. A big operation. Tell us what you know about this. Your vehicles were found there!" he huffed.

"I honestly don't know what you're talking about." she pleaded. "I do know the house." Tess admitted, "Evan wanted to buy it. A friend of his was leasing it. But, I wasn't interested in it. I thought it was over-priced. Evan was lease-purchasing the house next door to it for his son who has just started college at Kennesaw and ..." she faded off, her mind churning. Agent Broward cocked his head, his eyes still focused on her.

"The houses in that neighborhood weren't selling." she mumbled. "Evan was doing what?" she asked confused.

She sat staring blankly at the agent. A smirk slowly came across his face and she noticed a toothpick he had been chewing on, now secured in his mouth's corner. His cell phone rang and he answered,

"Broward!" He paused and growled, "Don't move!" as he walked into the middle section of the house to take this important call.

Tess's cell phone lay innocently on the table. She quickly slid it into her jeans pocket and turned to see Broward pacing back and forth, talking and grunting.

"On my God!" she thought. Her heart beating out of her chest. All kinds of things played through her mind. She knew Evan often had access to pot if he wanted it, but he didn't smoke it at all. He was very squeaky clean in that regard.

He was a pretty decent guy...no porno, strip clubs, drinking, cursing, smoking of any sort. He wasn't even into sports. He had a childhood friend he talked about who experimented and grew some marijuana in a closet until his mother found out...but that was it. Nothing like this.

A lot of his worker friends in the remodeling business drank and some smoked marijuana recreationally, but that was all she knew.

Broward returned to the table and loomed over her. "Ok, so are you ready to explain a few things?" he jeered.

"I'll tell you what I can, but it won't be much." she replied meekly. "I am clueless. I still can't believe it..."

"Oh you better believe it! This has been a year-long investigation. Your boyfriend has been busy with his marijuana operation. He hardly even exists as far as the government is concerned! He was in your car, your tags, your insurance. And this property here, is it all in your name?" he asked.

"Well, yes it is. He said he had a tax lien from a long time ago and that's why we hadn't gotten married yet…he didn't want to bring that into a marriage…" she started to break down, her mind reeling.

"There was never a tax lien. It was all a lie. He used you and he was going to leave you." Broward said triumphantly.

"What?" she exclaimed. Another shocker. Her eyes began to well up with tears as she sat crumpled and wilted on the wooden chair.

Broward confidently explained, "He was planning to leave you. He said you spent too much money on horses, hair-dos and getting your fingernails done!"

Touche'! Chalk one up for Broward.

Tess sniffled and slumped, feeling like a scolded child. "But, I…" she tried to speak with Broward cutting her off.

"…he was going to leave you. He deposited thirty-thousand into one of his bank accounts just this week!" he said proudly. Broward stared at her.

"Oh, I see." She tried to compose herself, now realizing he was baiting her.

"Hold on. Get a grip." she told herself. "You know Evan loves you with all his heart. Sure, our relationship has been strained, but he would never say anything about 'hair-dos and fingernails' I never get my nails done!" She knew what the Agent was doing and decided to play into his game.

"Do you know who he was going to leave me for?" she innocently asked, sniffling.

"Uh, well, you don't need to be concerned with that! He deposited fifty-thousand into his bank accounts and said you were costing him too much money." She was starting to get mad now...insecure tears turning to anger.

"Was it thirty or fifty thousand?" she demanded. "Why don't you get your story straight! You know, I'm willing to tell you what I know, but Evan leads his own life. I'm sure there is an explanation to all this. If, and that's a big if...he was involved, he purposely kept it from me...just like his affair..."

"He used you little lady and doesn't care who he brings down." Broward crowed. "You better start talking or this could get ugly."

"Don't threaten me." Tess defended.

"It's not a threat, it's a fact! Now, who else is involved in this grow operation with Evan? I know you know."

"I've told you, I don't know anything about it."

"You got the houses for him, didn't you?" he grinned.

"No! Absolutely not!" she fought back. " He had a couple rental houses, we were working on a fixer upper, flip but…"

"Where are they!" he scowled, gritting his teeth and leaning in, eyes piercing hungrily, almost salivating on the table.

She retreated back. "I'm not going to speak further without an attorney."

"Ok, Ms. Sanderson. If that's how you want to play it." He grumbled.

"Do you have a search warrant? Do you have a legal right to just barge into my home?" she helplessly asked.

"Oh, we've got a search warrant coming…I'm just waiting to get the call that it was signed off by the judge. Meanwhile, you just stay where I can see you and I'm going to talk to your house guests over there."

Broward marched through the large archway and into the foyer where Frank and DeeDee sat nervously waiting, coasts still on, grocery bags surrounding them on the floor, the other officer hovering beside them waiting for next instructions from Broward.

"I'm calling an attorney." She called after him. He did not acknowledge, but instead informed his colleague, Johnson, a non-descript fellow who could go unnoticed anywhere, "She's not going to cooperate...wants to do this the hard way. Call C-Man Ryan and let him know we'll be bringing in another on this Cayce case. See where he's at and how soon he can get here."

She sat there in utter disbelief. Bring her in? What was he talking about? Where was Evan? What had happened? Oh my God!

Frank hollered over. "If you need an attorney, call Billy Pruitt." and recited the phone number, which he knew by heart. Tess struggled to remember the number. She keyed it in on her hidden phone, with her back to the other room and slowly crept out of the kitchen and into the living room, removed from the others. Hitting send, she leaned into a corner, still trying to hide what she was doing, in the shadows.

Her hands were shaking. After a few rings a friendly southern voice inquisitively asked, "Hello?" obviously not recognizing the number coming in on his personal cell number, particularly after business hours. Tess identified herself, gave a stammering run-down of the last hour of this nightmare that had just come crashing down on her and pleaded..."Please help me!"

The shrewd attorney stayed calm and cool and asked a few questions and then said not to worry, he'd come see me in jail, if it went that far. "That's what they said!" she cried. "They are taking me to jail!"

The Search is On
Three or four uniformed police officers entered the house and began to confer with Broward, still in the vaulted area of the middle of the home, pacing back and forth. He seemingly had forgotten about Tess who had returned to her spot at the kitchen table.

"You need to get your dogs contained before we start the search. Here's a copy of the search warrant." He growled, pushing the paper in front of her.

"I can put them in their crates," she offered. "My horses are..."

He cut her off. "Is there anyone here to take care of the animals?" he asked turning to Agent Johnson, standing like a shadow behind him. "I didn't know there would be all these animals here and those two roommates either."

"Frank and DeeDee can care for the animals. Or my neighbors..." Tess stammered, now fearing they were going to call in Animal Control.

"No, we don't need to get Animal Control out here. Not tonight." He grumbled. "How many horses are there?" he asked.

"Uh, five, and my dogs and Frank and DeeDee's dogs..." Tess responded.

"Those two are ok. They are cooperating." Broward announced to minion Johnson referencing Frank and DeeDee, still sitting, now with uniforms huddled around them, writing and taking notes.

"They can stay here. Take Miss Sanderson in and she'll find out this isn't some sort of thing like she's seen on TV..."

"What am I being charged with? What about my rights?" she cried, standing up in protest.

"You just sit down and stay put. Don't move until we tell you." he ordered. His phone went off again and he warned her before he headed back to the other group of officers congregating in the open foyer, "I told you this could go either way."

With the commotion ensuing and the sounds of her bedroom and office getting torn apart, the dogs having been placed in their own little jail cells in their crates on the back porch, she sat nervously trying to think. Tess was still alone in the kitchen, everyone else preoccupied with rifling through her belongings, her files, her life!

Evan had little piles of papers in his area beside the bed and his desk in his part of Tess' office room, adjacent to the bedroom. He was not the most organized person and so many times Tess had asked him to pick up after himself and clean up his junk pile beside the bed. Clothes, magazines, junk mail, receipts, a coffee cup from the morning before.

Tess' ritual of affection for him was to bring him his morning cup of Joe in bed, since she was always up before dawn to feed the horses and take the dogs out.

Always waking with a kiss and a smile, Evan would sit up and look out the bay window, the morning sunrise breaking through the trees a beam at a time. With a yawn and a stretch and a sleepy smile, pull her towards him for a kiss and then proceed to tell her how much he loved waking up here, how much he loved waking up to her and how lucky they were.

"I've never lived anywhere that truly felt like home." he confessed. "I've never been with a woman in my whole life that I know to be 'the one'...not until now. I appreciate you Tess and I appreciate our home every single day." She would purposely stop to take in the moment, to enjoy the fleeting time, take in the wonderful morning view, sitting on the edge of the bed, Evan's arm around her, sipping the steeping coffee.

The thought of her sweet Evan jolted her back to the stark reality and she hoped and prayed he didn't have anything incriminating in his junk pile or on his desk. "Of course not." she thought adamantly...but doubts crept in. What if these accusations were true? What else didn't she know about Evan and his friends?

Sure, many were hippie types because of their age, some rednecks, blue collar and country types...most harmless she thought. Evan didn't discriminate based on background or social status. With his bleeding heart and willingness to help pretty much anyone he could, she questioned his judgement and always trusting and trying to see the best in people. It often made her feel too judgmental and almost snobbish.

She was not as trusting and kept herself shielded for most of her life, with a very limited and close circle around her of her mother and her dogs, some work friends here and there. Evan had family here, he was raised here, he went to school here. He was very personable. He had many friends and associates from all walks of life.

The Methheads or alcoholics he didn't associate with. His more creative friends and professional acquaintances considered themselves wine and cigar aficionados, and some marijuana connoisseurs.

The marijuana advocates would often say, "You never see a pothead robbing a convenience store to buy pot!" (like a meth user would do in a crazed stupor and drug desperation).

It was common knowledge that oxycodone and methamphetamine were a more dire problem to be dealt with in this country. Much more than marijuana.

Evan didn't even smoke...anything. He was a naturalist...he would not take any type of pills, except for vitamins and they had to be Shackley. He wouldn't even take an aspirin! He drank wine. He was generous to a fault.

He was unorganized...probably had A.D.D....but those were his worst qualities. (The worst that Tess knew.) He was practically a Saint! And she was practically Mother Teresa!

Still unnoticed in the kitchen with all the commotion going on, Tess slipped out the door along the breakfast area onto the front porch that ran along the entire front of the house. She stood in a shadowy corner and quickly speed dialed her mother. Her Mom's voice was cheerful as always and the happiness to hear from her daughter was apparent each time Tess called.

"Hi there, Sweetie!" she gleamed, "To what do I owe this pleasure? It's not even Sunday for our regular call!"

"Mom! Mom! Listen." Tess whispered. "Can you hear me?"

"Yes, yes. Tessie what's wrong?" her mother's happy surprise now turned to alarm.

"Evan is in trouble. Big trouble. The police are here and they are taking me to jail too. I don't know what's happening exactly but I'm sneaking this call. They are searching the house."

Her mother uttered a few words and questions, but was cut short by Tess's paranoia. "I've got to go. They are taking me to the county jail. They have Evan. Frank and DeeDee are here with the animals. I love you!" She flipped her phone shut and peeked inside, scared the light of the phone in use could be seen and she would be caught! The coast was still clear.

She found her neighbor's number and dialed. Voice mail. She left a similar cryptic message, with a plea to please look in on the horses and dogs if they could.

"Hey! What are you doing? Who are you calling?" Broward yelled as he came out the door, discovering his "key witness" prisoner was no longer stil sitting at the kitchen table. "Um, my attorney!" she blurted out, lying. He confiscated her phone and checked the last numbers dialed.

"My neighbor and my mother." she confessed.

"This investigation is still in progress!" he huffed.

"You weren't trying to warn anybody were you?"

"No! Who would I warn? I don't even know what's going on?" she cried.

"Yeah, sure you don't" he said sarcastically. "Come inside here and Officer Ryan is going to take you in and I'll just take this!" he sniped, taking her cell phone hostage.

A female officer…a big-boned gal with hair pulled tightly back and a regal native America profile, approached her and instructed her she was going to pat her down in a search. "Anything in your pockets?" she blankly asked with a completely emotionless tone.

"Hold your arms out and spread your legs apart."

In less than 30 seconds, Tess was handcuffed and helpless, her rights stripped from her instantaneously.

The short Officer Ryan, with his military buzz cut and chiseled face which you couldn't wipe off the slight grin, was showing her the search warrant and asking her to verify her name, address and social security number.

Was this happening?

Dee and Frank still sat huddled together on the bench that was used to take off your boots before entering the rest of the house. Dee's eyes welling with tears as she mouthed the words, "I'm so sorry." She looked ever so disheveled and distraught. Frank called out as they led her out of the house.

"It'll be ok. We'll take care of the animals. Don't worry!"

Those were the last words she heard as she left her wonderful life, knowing it would never be the same, forever changed.

The Ride of Your Life
The back of the police car was at least a little bit comfortable, with the cushion of the seat a welcome respite from the wooden kitchen chair, even with her arms bound behind her. The night was cool and brisk. The cruiser floated out the winding gravel drive and into the darkness. The officer driving radio'd as he accelerated, obviously enjoying the power of the car and of his position.

As they headed farther and farther away from her home, Tess looked helplessly out the window and tried not to think too much about the handcuffs pulling at her small wrists, as she leaned back on her arms securely contained behind her. She attempted a more comfortable position, but there was none.

She reminded herself to breathe and try to stay calm, telling herself that, like Frank had promised, everything was going to be ok. They would find out she didn't know anything about some grow house. She was sure it was one of Evan's friends, not him! But, what if he was involved? If he was, then surely they couldn't arrest *her* for something *he* was doing.

But he was in her car. "No! No! No! Stop this!" she told herself. "They can't do this!" (but they did!)

"They didn't even read me my rights!" (This isn't like TV)

I guess they do things differently in Cherokee County Georgia!

She thought back about the dually truck and her horse trailer...

She attempted to divert her thoughts by trying to identify where she was exactly, as houses and farms passed her in flashes and the cruiser cruised steadily ahead. They turned at the familiar Hickory Flat intersection which had been the topic of speculation as developers had been circling the area like buzzards, buying up farms and turning them into subdivisions of Mcmansions all huddled together on their postage stamp sized lots.

Wal-mart had tried to strong arm its way into this small community that now found it's place in an unwanted spotlight of desirability. Wally World had gotten shot down by zoning ordinances and opposition, but they would be back. The behemoth had a reputation for not backing down whether the community wanted them or not.

"The land in Cherokee County is so beautiful, no wonder everyone wants to be here." she thought.

It had given her a good platform for doing horse farms as her real estate niche and it wasn't far from neighboring Alpharetta. She realized the county was still rural, smalltown and still backward, but it was turning fast. Price point of most subdivision homes were half a million and up. There were a handful of golf course developments with several notable Atlanta Braves and Falcons as residents. Prices per acre started at $50,000. Atlanta suburban sprawl was coming fast and furious and North was super desirable.

Tess knew the area, but not all too well as she had only been here a year. As they encroached upon the city limits of the sleepy little hick town of Canton, they wound around the maze of city streets adjacent to Main with old brick buildings from the former mill town, now antique shops, thrift shops, an old convenience "stop n go" that had closed at 10:00 p.m. but still had the evil gambling Georgia Lottery neon lights beckoning any poor hopefuls who would throw away what little they had on scratch off tickets week after week.

Old row houses sat like dominos close to the curb, each a carbon copy to the next, remnants of an era gone by when the town had a thriving milling and textile trade.

Now they were run down breeding grounds for drugs, prostitution or just plain poverty.

Probably what few Blacks living in this mostly White, Puritan Redneck county, or the ever growing and thriving Hispanic community, lived in these little shacks and supported the Whites in the blue collar, fast food and landscaping jobs nobody else wanted.

The little ol' City of Canton, trying its darnedest to keep up with the county's growth, but unfortunately look liked a pubescent fourteen-year-old trying to look more mature in her older sisters make-up and clothes, only being able to pull of pathetic in the process.

They careened around a sharp curve, Tess' body sliding into the door, unsteady and unable to balance. Past another desolate, decrepit shopping center, now only for the Spanish with all signage in their native tongue.

Up a hill and then down as the cruiser made its way past a poultry processing plant to the Cherokee County Adult Detention Center.

Bright lights like those of a baseball field in full play regalia illuminated the horizon and the sharp turn at the Adult Detention Center and Animal Control sign sent Tess sliding again over to the other side in the back of the car.

The Officer Robot Driver in brown with the seeming power of God himself, radio'd of his impending arrival with his "One White Female" captive for the desolate and quietly cold Wednesday night.

They stopped at a giant metal gate and waited. Tess righted herself and looked at the large concrete building surrounded by chain link and razor wire spooled along the top. The gate rolled slowly open at the sound of a buzz, then another. As the patrol car lurched through, the gates made their slow return to the tightly secured position.

Whipping around a motor lobby like that of a hospital emergency room intake, the car stopped on a dime. Roughly shoving it into park and turning the engine off, the officer quickly was at her door and helped her out. The irony of the chivalry struck her.

Through the automatic "intake" door, he directed her through an open area with rows of seats connected together in the center, desks and counter areas to the right like those at the DMV with several officers busy with the paperwork or talking amongst themselves.

The flourescent lights were stark and blaring, giving everyone a pale yellow tinge. Her eyes squinted trying to adjust and the officer directed her to a small group of the same utilitarian chairs against the wall next to a metal door.

"Hold up here Ma'am" the officer gestured in a sweet southern tone. This was the first time she had heard the burly fellow speak. She waited.

He immediately replaced the tootsie pop he had been nursing, the white stick now returning to it's rolling from side to side. He ambled down the hallway and through another door that banged loudly as it swung shut. Tess could see his reappearance at the desks lining the large open area.

Two female officers were now upon her, opening the metal door next to her and motioning for her to come in. One observed as the other mechanically unlocked her handcuffs as Tess stood inside a barren room, the same municipal creamy off-white as the rest of the Detention Center, with only a folding table on one wall and a lone plastic chair sitting off to one side.

Tess searched the officer's faces noticing how normal they looked...one a White woman in her 50s with a sweet face and glasses...someone's mother and probably a grandmother she thought. She looked too prim and proper to be a Deputy, but she was.

The other was a Black woman with a stern look, one void of expression on purpose...probably in her mid 30s with beautiful skin, likely mixed with Cherokee Indian in her ancestry as told by her lighter tone. The contrast of the brown uniform only enhanced her.

Their gun belts were filled with their weapons...gun, pepper spray, night stick, handcuffs and the woven black leather creaked as they moved. Tess wondered if the first officer, Morris her shining name badge read, could even shoot her gun, let alone wrestle any one down if she had to. She seemed pretty harmless. Now the other one, with the stone expression...she wasn't so sure about her.

She was instructed to remove her clothes.
Her jeans were cuffed and when told to fold the cuff down, stall shavings from her barn work cascaded onto the spotless tile floor.

Her boots were dusty and with traces of mud engrained in the soles.

Her undershirt, a cotton turtle neck, was still damp with sweat and her favorite, throw-on nylon navy blue Sear's coat with that unmistakable orange lining, her trusty barn-coat, soiled and dusty, ready to get thrown into the wash at any time now. That orange would soon haunt her.

"I'm sorry if I smell like a horse." she apologized. "I was in my barn before they..."

"Take your shoes and socks off, your bra and underwear and stand facing the wall." Officer Morris ordered. Tess complied, shivering facing the wall. The other officer, wearing rubber gloves, placed her removed clothing into a large plastic zip lock bag and remained silent.

"Now squat and cough three times." Morris instructed.

Naked and cold, in the complete and stark light, fully exposed, she complied.

Satisfied that she wasn't hiding anything in her rectum after the squat, she was then instructed to turn around and was handed an orange canvas top and pants.

"What's your shoe size?"
A pair of matching orange slip on rubber sandals were produced.

Tess quickly put on the prison uniform. She was freezing. She slipped on the sandals.

"Can I keep my underwear and bra?" she asked hopefully.

"Can I keep my socks?" but was rebuffed each time with a stern and unsympathetic "No" which she couldn't understand.

"Sit here." she was ordered and left sitting in the empty room in the lone chair, in her bright orange scrubs covering her complete nakedness underneath.

The CCADC: More Intake
She took a deep breath, crossed her arms and hugged herself trying to get some warmth despite the chill in the stark room. She pulled her knees to her chest, bowed her head and closed her eyes. The blackness was an envelope of comfort.

In what seemed like an instant, but could have been thirty-minutes or longer, Officer Morris was back with a piece of paper and summoning Tess to come with her now.

"This is your personal property list of what you came in with." she informed.
1 blue jacket, 1 green turtleneck, 1 green sweater, 1 pair of blue pants, 1 pair of green socks, 1 pair pink underwear, 1 pink bra, 1 pair of boots.

"Sign this page." she ordered producing a duplicate. "You keep that one."

They entered an open room next to the intake area and now Tess could see multiple of glassed-in rooms, narrow and stark, to the left, placed across the room from the officer's work stations so anyone contained therein could be plainly viewed. Some were dark, others were lit.

She was led around to the left towards them. As she made her way past the first holding room that was dark, she saw sitting on the concrete bench facing her in the next was Evan!

Still in the clothes she remembered him in from earlier that day...the luminescent turquoise blue polo shirt, one of her favorite colors on him that really brought out his striking features of dark almost black hair and those hypnotic green eyes...and of course his black jeans that he preferred always.

He was sitting with his legs crossed Indian-style, head bowed. He raised his head slightly and turned his eyes to Tess's as she walked past. Words can hardly convey what those eyes said, the sadness, the complete and utter sorrow, and the deep circles underneath a testament to the strain he must have been under since early that afternoon.

Their eyes locked in that fleeting moment. She felt pain in her heart and was forced to take a quick breath. There he was...the love of her life. There she was... in a prison uniform being paraded by him as calculated leverage.

Her holding cell was at the end of the row of rooms, giving her a view towards the entrance. She could see the officer's work area and desks clearly and officers moving about.

She watched the lite flow of activity for a minute, standing up, walking back and forth and then sitting again on that cold stone concrete bench.

A couple of Mexicans were called from the seating area in the middle of the room, over to the counters. The television blared with some non-descript sportscast on ESPN and she just noticed the sound of it above all the thoughts racing through her mind and her heart beating out of her chest.

She was up and down and then down again trying to calm herself. "This is what the Detective's want. They are trying to use you as bait to lure Evan into a confession of guilt." she thought.

"Why wasn't he in a prison uniform?" she wondered.

"Had they threatened him? Been rough with him?" she worried.

He was a strong man, but a very passive and kind soul.

That look he gave her would be etched in her mind for eternity.

"God, I hope he is ok." she prayed.

"Breathe. Breathe." she instructed herself. "Be calm. You didn't do anything wrong. You've never even had a traffic ticket in your whole life!"

"Breathe." She closed her eyes and tried, but that lasted only seconds. Her eyes were back open wide looking out her limited view, to try to get a clue as to what was happening
.

She watched as Evan was led out of the holding cell. Then again as he was returned in *his* orange uniform. Several other men in theirs were escorted to the middle holding area and sat intently watching the TV set above that droned on. Waiting.
She stood and leaned against the thick glass window of the metal door, looking out, staring blankly still telling herself to "breathe." Feeling Evan's presence only a few feet away, but world's away, surrounded by security and cinder block walls.

Tess sighed and sat down again. Her neck was tight and in knots, and she really had to go to the bathroom. How long had it been she wondered?

She didn't even realize that at the back of the holding cell was a half wall with a stainless steel toilet attached to a stainless steel sink with push-button water controls that send water up in a small arc like a water fountain.

In the side of the stainless cylinder base between the sink and where the toilet attaches was a round toilet paper roll opening that was empty. "It figures." she shrugged.

A metal plate was attached to the wall above the sink, mirror height and Tess studied her warped reflection. "Forty-years old...never been in trouble my whole adult life. What am I doing here?"
"You look pretty good, all things considered!" she mused.

Tess was lucky. Good genes. All the women in her family were healthy and hearty and could easily pass for 10 years younger than their true age. And if it ever came up...that impromptu question of age that most women avoid like the plague...she was happy to say "pushing 40" because of the reaction of disbelief it brought.

For whatever reason, she thought of that now. The tinge of vanity interrupted by the reminder that she needed to go to the bathroom!

She checked the vantage point from the commode behind the half wall barrier. It appeared that only her knees could possibly be visible if she squatted over the bowl. Luckily there was a big square pole blocking the last officer's desk across the room and the other inmates watching TV in the center were out of view.

She marveled at the geometrics of whoever designed the place as she held her squat over the bowl, careful not to let her skin touch it. Her thighs burned. She automatically reached for toilet paper but was reminded that the roll was empty.

"Great! No toilet paper. No underwear. No socks. My feet are freezing. I've got a headache." she grumbled to herself.

"Well, I guess these should be the least of my worries!" she laughed, returning to her seat on the cold, hard concrete bench.

Movement caught her eye as she looked up from her bowed-head position, having been trying to help her headache and release some tension from the knotted neck muscles. She saw some activity and a large man with sandy hair and beard in fleeting images through a small square observation type window. A baritone voice issued muffled utterances and seemed to resonate through the floor like a low rumble. It somehow sounded familiar. She strained to see and then sat back down after a few minutes of nothing.

Eyes closed, head down trying to "feel" Evan...trying somehow to make a connection with him. It wasn't working. Too much stress and anxiety...the tension going from her temples to her neck and shoulders. She couldn't quiet her mind as thoughts continued to whirl round and round. Her head throbbed.

Another inmate was brought in through the automatic door, male officers on either side and one behind. A very large man. Big, burly, but not obese. She understood why there were three officers to the one. He looked like a Norseman with his tussled and wild head of reddish blonde hair, and well-trimmed but longer full beard and moustache.

He shuffled steadily, arms forward, handcuffed, shoulders relaxed...not a threat to anyone. As they approached Tess's holding cell, he glanced up. The despair in the crystal blue eyes peering out from under the frame of thick brows was undeniable.

Their eyes locked for the 1/2 dozen steps it took him to pass her "window" and then the sound of keys, a thud and echo, reverberations of the metal door closing after his striking image disappeared.

The sound of the droning TV returned, having been muted in her mind as her attention was drawn to the new inmate and everything had gone into a surreal dream-state moving in slow motion. She felt like she was in a movie.

"Holy Moly!" she said out loud. "Or more appropriately Holy Shit!" she chided herself.

Visions of her Grandmother came front and center. "Why should I watch my language now? I'm in jail!" She mused and then let out a "Ha!" and sat down again with a thud and an "ouch" forgetting how hard the concrete bench was.

"Damn!" she exclaimed. "Damn! Damn! Damn!" rubbing her head still pounding and throbbing like Stomp! the Musical, which also incidentally gave her a headache.

Brian and Diana

"Brian" she thought. Some pieces of the puzzle started coming into place. Brian had become a fast friend of Evan's recently. They were introduced by a mutual friend and quickly found many things in common. Both had grown up in Marietta and they were close in age. Their high schools had been staunch rivals. Brian was a defensive linebacker on his football team and someone no one could get past at 6'5" and 300 pounds!

Evan had been in the band drum corps and held lead position right out of the gate his freshman year which was unheard of and a first! He went to all the games, of course, with the band and the two guys reminisced about their glory days over beers and wings, finding out "It was you! who stole the mascot!" And remember when "Junior Simms brought those greased pigs and let them loose in the halls!"

...Running up the opposing schools flag on their flag pole, big parties, rivalries, fights and rumbles, how it wasn't a big deal to drive to school in your pick-up with gun racks and their shotguns proudly displayed and no one gave it a second thought. Those were the days!

They both had grown up and were witness to the disappearance of farm land in the once rural Cobb County, being replaced by subdivisions and shopping centers and anything else anyone could build for profit. Evan's family had sold their land at the base of Kennesaw Mountain years before and he was always nostalgic whenever they drove by that area or talked about it, wishing he still had some of the family's land left to him, but it just hadn't worked out that way.

Evan told Tess stories about how he would ride his pony, Frisky, all over the foothills of the mountain and historic Civil War battlefield, now a national park. And how the little pony would make a game of trying to get him off his back any way possible. Once the pony had made his point, there would be no more games as the boy and his trusty steed would explore the forests and streams, spending all their days of Summer on this magical mountain.

His family were salt of the earth, Baptist folks. Farmers. Dirt poor, but proud people. He fondly remembered his grandparents with much love and adoration of their good, solid lives, spirituality and perseverance.

Brian, Evan excitedly told Tess, had been a pro-wrestler some years before on the circuit with some celebrity and fanfare. Now the big scary dude (with the resulting back problems from years of bodily abuse) was on a different circuit!

Brian competed in a different game...one with cards, chips and bets...working on making a name for himself on the Poker circuit. A gambler with his fair share of luck, he also had a landscape business and Evan had spoken to Tess about the prospect of becoming a partner in it with him. There were a few commercial accounts he already had and Evan could get more, along with servicing the farm and the couple rental houses. It sounded like a good opportunity and that was the purpose of their first meeting.

Tess remembered that first meeting at the Sushi Bar in Kennesaw. He rode up on a Harley decked out in leather. A sight you couldn't miss, heralded by the roar of the bike! As he ambled in to the restaurant, helmet in hand, red-gold hair slicked back, the big grin on his face jolly and infectious...he wasn't so scary after all!

His large form easily filled up the whole other side of the booth. Tess and Evan happily sitting side by side on theirs as they always did, whether someone else was joining them or not! Just another syrupy-sweet thing some couples do.

Tess quickly found out that the big, scary biker dude, former pro-wrestler turned pro-poker player was really a big teddy bear who loved his mother, was a gentleman who didn't cuss and had a heart of gold.

A true Southern boy that was proud of his heritage but progressive enough in his thinking to not hold any racial prejudices and even would tolerate sushi! She liked him immediately. He excitedly told them that he had just gotten a gig to play Santa Claus at the Children's Hospital and would also be handing out all the Toys for Tots during a big run the local Harley riders were planning in the coming holiday months. "I've got the red suit already." he boasted. The unmistakable glint in his eye just like St. Nick's younger brother that just so happened to prefer Harley horsepower to reindeers.

It was a lively lunch at the trendy Rusan's with techno music pulsing over the cascading din of the patrons. A place like this in Kennesaw? It was a little odd...a little too progressive...but maybe the area was developing and outgrowing its confederate, KKK persona of decades past. Maybe.

Evan and Brian excitedly made plans for the landscape company, talking about rolling in Evan's remodeling work. Tess was so glad that he would have a worthy partner, having not really approved of most of Evan's friends or subs.

Brian spoke of "the love of his life." A woman named Diana and they all promised they would get together for dinner very soon.

When Tess first met Diana, she was totally caught off guard. They had been invited to Brian and Diana's place for dinner the following weekend. They lived in a townhome in a bustling area of Marietta, not far from the quaint Marietta Square and notable train depot. The townhome was decorated in all the latest colors and schemes, with beautiful draperies and designer accents throughout. Tess made a mental note of this immediately.

Brian greeted them and showed them in, cooking noises coming from the galley kitchen behind the living room wall. The aroma of something really good welcomed them. The dining table was set and looked beautiful with a lace table cloth and lovely china arranged just so. The Nautilus equipment looming over from the corner was obviously Brian's and obviously out of place.

A petite woman with a kind face and rosy cheeks from the heat of the kitchen came hurriedly out from behind the wall to greet her guests. Wiping her hands with a towel, she smiled sweetly. Introductions were made and drink orders were taken. Sweet tea. Unsweet. Diet Coke. Water.

Diana sure wasn't what Tess expected. She expected some type of Biker Babe and got Biker Grandma or maybe more appropriately Mrs. Santa Claus instead! They were seated in the living room while Brian and Diana retreated into the galley. It seemed like they really hadn't done that much entertaining...either because of lack of space or lack of inclination. But they were excited to have their guests today.
Evan squeezed Tess's hand and they smiled at each other. He leaned over to kiss her softly has he often did. This was a nice change for them to be doing something as a couple, with another couple. Schedules had kept them too busy for socializing much as of late.

Tess whispered in his ear, "Diana isn't what I pictured!" Evan smiled and squeezed her hand, "Oh, she's great."

The little lady...probably no more than five feet tall, resembled a librarian or schoolmarm with her hair pulled back in a bun, complete with wire-rimmed glasses. She was animated and funny as she talked happily about her family...her sisters, her daughter, her grandchildren who's framed pictures could be found dotted throughout the now noticeably overstuffed space.

She taught children's Sunday School sometimes, worked as a secretary at an architectural firm and had a very full life. Tess was intrigued by how this big bear of a biker dude and the demure little librarian of a woman could have possibly gotten together.

Opposites attract as they say. Diana told "their" story of how Brian and her husband had been best friends. "He was always over at the house hanging out. We've known each other for over 15 years." Her husband died from health problems...she found him dead in their bathroom. Brian had been the dutiful best friend to him and then Diana after his passing. Their friendship and unexpected romance bloomed as the result of the shared grief. It was a sad story.

Tess smiled at the two of them...Diana the mother hen, bossing big Brian around and he willingly and ever so earnestly wanting to please her. They were really cute together, she concluded.

As it usually did with Tess and Evan, the conversation eventually turned to real estate. She shared her recent career path with an interested Diana and the topic made its way to their rental house that was still in the process of being renovated.

"It's an awesome house." Tess explained. "We just ran out of money."

"We'll get it finished. Things just take longer than you think. It's always something, you know?" Evan added.

"I can help you decorate if you need it." Diana offered.

"Oh, I would love that! I'm so challenged in that department! Especially picking paint colors and curtains. You've done such a great job with this space!" Tess complimented her.

"It was ok when it was just me." Diana confessed. "But when Brian moved in...well, you can see we're crammed for space."

As the conversation progressed, Diana and Brian agreed to go have a look at the rental house and see if they could help finish the renovations and get the place ready to sell or just rent it themselves. It didn't matter to Tess. She was just happy "something" was going to happen with the place. It had been sitting all summer and was becoming a bone of contention between her and Evan.

Tess's mother had gotten the loan for it...as an investment...since Tess already had a mortgage tying up her credit. Evan had taken it over as a lease/purchase and had struggled with getting it completed.

Tess leveraged her credit with Home Depot and went overboard with a dream kitchen, which was absolutely fabulous by the way, but probably too much for the house and for the neighborhood.

Evan wanted to do granite counters...the kind with rose quartz in it. The walls were taken out to give it a better flow and open concept to the vaulted great room. The bathrooms were to be redone and the flooring replaced. It was a cedar contemporary from the late 70s, about to be brought into the 21st Century! Sitting wounded and forlorn, this foreclosure patiently waiting to be brought back to life.

Originally, it was planned to be Evan and Tess's first home together, in addition to their first real estate venture. That's why some of the rehab work was so over the top...like the kitchen...because they thought they were going to be living there themselves! Then Tess got back into horses...something she didn't plan at all...got tired of living in the construction zone, the house still ripped apart, Evan's A.D.D. just beginning to come to light.

After starting working with Bob, Tess just went out and got her OWN horse farm, leaving the contemporary money pit behind.

She was more than happy to offer it to Brian and Diana and looked forward to seeing it put back together and what Diana could do with it, if they decided to take it after all.

Her mind was still reeling. What was Brian doing here? How could he have been involved? What had he and Evan been up to? Brian was a gambler, admittedly. But even with his "outlaw" appearance, she had found was more of a facade and alter-ego, like whatever character he played when he was a wrestler. Granted, she had not known him or Diana very long, but she would bet that he was a straight arrow. Diana definitely was!

The Bleeding Hearts Club Band

So many questions. No answers, only speculation. Fear. Anxiety. Paranoia. Sadness. Concern. What had these guys gotten themselves (and her and Diana into)? Which acquaintance of Evan's had used him as a fall guy to save themselves? Some Methhead Bodyman from his distant past, or a Crackhead Painter from one of the rehab jobs. Evan knew his fair share of undesirables, but always spoke of the goodness in a person's heart, overlooking their vices.

She had been witness to Evan's bleeding heart time and again and tried to put her foot down. Evan absolutely refused to not offer assistance to anyone who asked him. She tried to stress that "charity begins at home," but he wouldn't hear her. Whether it was his Mother, Sister, ex-Wife, Son, Neice, ex-girlfriend 1, ex-girlfriend 2, former school friend 1, former school friend 2, sub 1 or sub 2, and so on, he was always on call to help.

At first Tess didn't like it at all, but had to understand the maintenance of the relationship with the ex-wife, because of his son and respected him for manning up to those responsibilities. He was the only man left in the family to aide his Mother and Sister, she respected him for that too. It was just hard. Always feeling like second, third or even fourth place. Always back burner. Taken for granted.

Tess remembered hearing about a guy Evan worked with who had been put in jail for Methamphetamine. This fellow was probably desperate. It could have been him? She shook her head in disbelief still trying to sort it all out. She could guess all night.

Staring in awe out the window of the cell, another familiar face was lead past. It was Diana! She too in all her orange glory! Her hair that had been meticulously pulled back and neat to the extreme was now a wild rat's nest jutting straight up and out revealing it's length and coarse texture. Her small form hung the large boxy orange top, probably two sizes too big to accommodate her large chest. It was almost down to her knees!

Her eyes glared through her coke bottle glasses that only amplified the look of fear and shock. Her once colorful and friendly face, now a pale chaulky mask, void of expression.

Tess carefully kept watch out her plexiglass window. She could only see straight across the room to general intake and the waiting area, with limited angles up the hall, even if she pushed her face up against the glass.

She saw Evan again taken out and then brought back in his orange uniform. She saw him taken over to the desks and information exchanged, then returned again to the holding cell out of view. Then it was her turn to be checked in.

Tess was escorted from her holding cell by the Black female officer, who said little and wouldn't even acknowledge her, look at her. "Come this way." she instructed.

At the intake desk she was presented with the paperwork of her charges which stated what she was charged with, "Manufacturing marijuana - 300 plants!" a felony with a bond of $350,000!

"What in the world?" she questioned out loud.

"How can I be charged for something so ridiculous! I wasn't there! I had no knowledge. How an they do this? This has got to be a really big mistake!" she cried to deaf ears. Neither officer acted like they heard her say anything at all.

"Don't I get a phone call?" she stammered at the Black female officer standing guard. "Go with him." she blankly motioned. "We need your photo taken."

Tess was handcuffed to a robotic officer and led over to an area at the end of the row of desks. She was uncuffed and then ushered into place, instructed to stand still, like getting her driver's license, but she wasn't smiling. This was a mug shot! What was happening? Was this really happening?

Visions flashed in her mind of her, Evan's, Diana's and Brian's pictures on the local news looking like derelicts, as the photos always do...with the announcer saying "A large marijuana manufacturing operation busted...local Realtor arrested..." she shuddered at the thought.

And then came the fingerprinting, but not like anything she'd ever seen on TV. It must have been a newer machine. There was no ink! It scanned each fingertip and the fingerprints appeared on the screen and were checked for clarity, then saved to her file.

She watched curiously as the guard, with the personality of a slug, another drone, offered only directives without expression or emotion which seemed the norm.

It was pretty amazing seeing this technology firsthand...definitely not something she ever thought of in her wildest dreams would hold her complete unique information.

As she stood at the fingerprinting scanner, a list of names and dates appeared on the screen...of the prior hands whose fingerprints had been received. Her eyes immediately were drawn to a familiar name...a name she knew! A construction worker friend of Evan's, Chris Cole, fingerprinted two weeks prior it said. What did that mean? Could he have been part of all this?

The White female offer, who she started with, came over to where she stood and handed the fingerprinting officer a separate document which he looked over and then presented to Tess. "They've added another charge." he announced blandly.

"Trafficking...possession of over ten pounds of marijuana. That one's not bondable."

"Possession! Trafficking! Over ten pounds!" she cried. "This is ridiculous!"

"Don't I get a phone call? I need to contact my attorney!"

"Just have a seat here Ma'am." he directed as he finished up her fingerprint file and inputting the charges. She stood there in shock, unable to move.

"Have a seat, Ma'am." She sat. Staring. Numb. Tired. Cold. Confused. Still trying to sort out this unfolding nightmare that just kept getting worse.

She looked up to see Evan being led past her, coming from getting "his" mug shot. He looked a little bit better than he had before. Their eyes met and he mouthed the words, "I love you."

Nightmare on Cherokee Street

Tess just stared and watched as he was led through a separate door that closed with a loud locking thud echoing throughout the space. She wondered when she'd ever see him again, sitting there blinking blindly.

"Ok Sanderson!" she was jolted back to the here and the now, her mind somewhere in nothingness. The officer motioned her up with a "Let's go." and herded her down an opposite hallway that looked like everywhere else she'd seen so far. Fluorescently illuminated, so bright sunglasses would be welcome.

She looked at the non-descript door I.D.s for any clues, but there were only numbers.

Then they were buzzed through another door and then another, through another. Then a quick left to an area with utilitarian chairs, like a small waiting area, another bank of holding cells and a glassed in office area...all dim because of the time now 2:00 or 3:00 in the morning. Then through two more sets of locked doors.

The officer called codes on the walkie-talkie perched just below his ear on his shoulder, tilting his head slightly to the side as he talked. This communication buzzed them through again, the automatic locking mechanisms clicking into place behind them.

"Go to your right." he ordered.

As she turned right, her eyes followed the length of the corridor before her which went on and on and on and on. She almost did a double-take trying to see if there were any mirrors involved in creating this illusion. It was like the hall in Disney's Haunted Mansion. It went on forever!

She fully expected "Michael" or "Freddy" or "Jason" to pop out at any moment. The thought amused her slightly as she trudged on, one plastic sandaled foot in front of the other, into this new unknown Nightmare on Cherokee Street.

They passed several marked doors..."Attorney Visitation," "Law Library," "Food Services," "Storage Room A23" "A25" "A27." After what seemed an eternity, she was instructed to "Hold up."

More walkie-talkie communication and another set of doors buzzed open and they entered a dull foyer area of grey concrete with two other hallways immediately to the right and the left and two windows and doors with tinted glass so you could not see through.

As the door shut loudly behind them, she stood looking at her full-length reflection in the glass before her. For the first time since this ordeal had begun, she was now witness to all her jailhouse glory. She just blankly stared.

It was completely silent like the whole world was holding its breath waiting for something to happen. She felt like she was deep underground, devoid of the world above.

A majorly butch female officer came through the door in front of them. She conversed briefly with the other officer, and he quickly and quietly retreated "into the light."

This female officer took androgyny to a new level. Tess immediately thought of the SNL character Pat, who no one could quite tell for sure if she was a she or a he. This gal was a woman she guessed, only because of her charge of the female inmates. Her hair was military cut on the sides and back, with sprigs on top, spiked up like a crown.

Her face was not feminine, or friendly. She gruffly instructed Tess to get a plastic bin stacked on the wall behind her in the shadows, originally unnoticed. Tess complied.

The guard opened one of the interior doors and produced a bed roll...a plastic coated mat, not too far off from the one Tess used for yoga! "Take this too." she ordered. Tess put the bin under one arm and clutched the folded mat as best she could with her other hand, half-way dragging it along as she was led into the Pod.

The room was dimly lit and so quiet that every movement they made was amplified ten times and reverberated. It was a two-story triangular space with numbered doors on two of the elongated walls on lower and upper levels. She noticed the picnic style stainless tables and attached stools that filled the open floor, empty, waiting. They passed several shower stalls, 3-sided concrete boxes to the left and the guard stopped at door number 1, the keys rattling as she opened it.

Tess's heart began beating faster like a drum roll in anticipation, images flashing through her mind of what might await her behind door number 1. A strange image like a Russ Meyer film of "Broads in the Big House" or of scowling buxom bleach blondes with cigarettes hanging from their bottom lips mocking her..."Hey there girlie girl!"...flashed. The taunts in her mind quickly silenced as she entered the room...her new reality.

Two metal bunks were attached to the back wall of the 15' x 8' box. A metal desk top and small round seat attached on the wall next to a small shelf with dull clothes hooks. The toilet sink combo with the same stainless steel square of a mirror mimicked her holding cell decor.

Once two steps in the room with her bin and bed roll in hand, the door was closed with a loud bang that made her jump, with no regard for the sleeping and quiet in the early morning hours.

She gingerly placed her new belongings on the floor and just stood there, helplessly yearning for this to be over, not knowing if was only the beginning.

"Don't you dare cry!" she ordered herself silently. She thought it strange that she didn't feel like she was falling apart. Maybe on some subliminal level she knew it wasn't an option. She had to be strong.

"It's going to be ok." she told herself, placing the bed pad on the lower metal bunk. She sat there in silence.

Interruptions from the officer's walkie talkie came in burps and blips, causing ripples in the night's hibernation. She rubbed her eyes and temples, the pain and throbbing still present, just momentarily forgotten. The sound of keys at her door brought her back to the present and the he-she officer ordered her to "get your stuff and come on." with a hint of aggravation in her tone.

"What's happening?" Tess asked innocently.

"They need to make up their cotton-pickin' minds." the officer grumbled.
Cotton-pickin'? Did she really just say that?

Tess dutifully "got her stuff" and followed the officer back out the way she had come and down the long hallway to door "M138," through a luminescent maze of cinder blocks painted of butter into another wing of the sprawling detention facility.
She kept her eyes peeled for any sign of Evan, Brian or Diana. Nothing. No one. The brightly lit hallways completely barren.

This new area she was being led to was obviously a medical facility with file holders on doors, gurneys in the hall, curtained-off examining area and two lone nurses in scrubs at a half-octagon nurses desk.

Tess was put into a room with a sliver view of the nurse's station diagonally across the corridor. This room was similar to her last but with only one bed. She was thankful for the privacy and put the bed roll on the metal platform.

She explored the contents of the now infamous plastic bin. There she found a brown canvas bed cover or sack and a brown sheet so thinly woven you could almost see through it. Completing the sleep ensemble, an orange cotton throw that was to be her blanket.
She laid the sheet over the bed pad and covered herself with the canvas sack and throw. She always liked the heaviness of a quilt, layered with another blanket at home. The canvas gave it some weight and helped make things warmer in general. It wasn't too cold in the room, but not very comfortable either.

As she lay there, she tried to let her body generate warmth. No socks. No underwear. No bra. She folder her arms around herself and laid still. She did not want to move for fear of losing any of her "heat." She lay still like a moth in her cocoon.

"Breathe." she told herself. "Try to relax." She noticed she was one tight wad of muscles in knots...from the still pounding, pulsing headache, down her neck, all the way down her spine. She tried desperately to release the tension she had been holding for hours and closed her eyes.

She ordered her mind, going 100 miles per hour, to "Stop!" She rubbed her head, then her neck.

"Ooooohhh!" she quietly moaned. "And this bed is so uncomfortable." she felt the unwieldy metal beneath the pad like the foam was not even there. With a big sigh, her eyes closed. She sheilded them from the glare of the overhead florescent light with the top blanket, a soothing darkness enveloping her and instaneous release and sleep came.

In her subconscious she floated heavily into a deep black hole in some other realm. It was quiet there. Weightless. Nothingness. Blank. She was in some type of suspended animation brought on by the duress. Time didn't move. It seemed like an infinite duration but could have been only minutes. Tess couldn't tell.

Girl Interrupted: Morning Comes
The sound of a radio playing country music and voices echoing, laughing, of women chatting and carrying on brought her back to the desolate cell.

She opened her eyes under the cover. They almost seemed foggy from her breath. Batting the cover away like one would a spider's web you run into, she sat straight up listening.

Tossing the blanket and canvas cover to the side, she was at the window of the door straining to see out of the small window. A couple of young girls in white "inmate workforce" uniforms were standing at the nurses station...of which one corner she could see. They leaned on brooms and chatted with a nurse in a blue uniform who looked to be of similar age.

Tess watched as they talked and then eventually went back to their work, the latest country hits giving background music to the scene.

Tess went back to the bed platform and tried desperately to resume her dream state, but it was no use. It must be morning now, predawn she presumed, with the level of active sounds increasing as moments passed.

She sat there listening, getting up to see what she could see out her little window on the door, then back into position...legs crossed, blanket wrapped around her like a shawl. Bowing her head to try to ease the pain of the still throbbing, still beating drum in her temples.

She paced, tried to stretch, leaning forward to touch her toes, her back and neck muscles resisting like an opponent in a tug-of-war game. She worried about her house, the animals, Evan...everything. She sat again and then got up at the sound of keys in her door and a face looking in through the sidelight.

An officer stood with a thick plastic tray and asked, "Do you want breakfast?"

"Uh, sure." she uttered, clearing her throat, it feeling strange to talk. The sound of her own voice foreign.

"Thank you." She said politely as she took the tray with both hands.

"Coffee?" asked a goober-looking "inmate workforce" fellow from the background, wearing a plastic hairnet, pushing a metal cart piled high with stacks of the multi-colored pastel trays.

"Oh yes!" Tess exclaimed. "Coffee would be wonderful!" she said gratefully and with anticipation.

"Cup!" the inmate ordered with a toothless smile, Tess now noticing the glint in his eye as he intently looked at her, which was embarrassing. She must have obviously looked confused standing there tray in hand, waiting to be served.

"Give him your cup." the officer directed, patience running thin as they were trying to make their morning rounds.

"...in your bin" he said with some irritation.

"Oh, oh..." she said shyly looking around, her hands full with the tray and nowhere to put it.

"Just put the tray on the sink." the officer offered, his voice softening slightly.

She did so and fumbled with the lid of the bin on the floor, quickly producing the small beige cup, proudly handing it to the inmate. He happily filled it with the brow liquid gold.

"There you are Ma'am." he said cordially with a sweet southern drawl.

Tess thanked him looking directly in his eyes. He looked bashfully back, then with a yearning as the door closed.

She turned and looked blankly at the tray teetering on the small sink above the attached commode. She tried a very tentative sip of the coffee. It smelled burnt. A repugnant taste of metal and something not even remotely resembling coffee, except the color, hit her taste buds hard. Tree bark and mud, boiled in a rusty pot, would have tasted better. She spit it out into the sink immediately...a spray of brown going all over the small bowl.

"Ahhhh!" she cried with a scowl across her face, wiping her mouth with the back of her hand. She dumped the coffee in the toilet, satisfied that was where it belonged.

She then eyed the tray with serious caution. Oatmeal in one of the larger squares with a packet of jelly, two pieces of white bread in another and two hard boiled eggs. The remaining small square with a carton of apple juice slyly concealing a small packet of salt and another of pepper.

"Well, everything's here." she said out loud, announcing to herself.

"Humm...no utensils or napkins." she observed, then turned to her trusty bin...three small bars of soap, a small toothbrush in a plastic sealed covering, but no toothpaste, one small mini-deodorant stick and a mini shampoo of the exclusive "Maximum Security" brand, which made her laugh out loud.

"Maximum Security shampoo and deodorant!" she mused tossing the travel-sized items back into the bin.

A brown handtowel and a rag of a matching washcloth tattered and stringy on all four sides. And, compliments of the county's Sheriff, a copy of the 16 page black and white copy pamphlet the "Official" Adult Detention Center Inmate Handbook"...so there will surely be no misunderstandings..."And, we hope you enjoy your stay!"

She flipped the pages, rolled her eyes, and tossed it back in. She rummaged through the remainder of her "welcome" items and found the yellow-mustard spoon with a small fork-like ridge at the end. Her trusty Spork! Bon appetite!

Tess grabbed the tray and almost dropped it, pulling her left hand back as if touching something super-hot...a gooey mess on her hand from the pasty oatmeal. No paper towels! How could she survive this!

She put the tray on the bed and quickly rinsed her hand, thankful for at least some water.

Fumbling again in the bin, she retrieved the handtowel and sat on the side of the bed looking at the tray, now taunting her. She tried to muster some bravery. She thought of the reality shows she'd seen where people had to eat all kinds of things in the competition...bugs, worms, animal organs considered to be delicacies in foreign lands.

"Compared to that, this isn't that bad," she tried to reassure herself.

"Or was it?' a voice inside her head warned, an image of african tribes dancing her sitting in the sand...tray in front..fire torches blazing in a circle around her...spears pointing at her, natives chanting..."Eat! Eat! Eat!"

She shook her head dissolving the image like shaking a snow globe and tentatively spooned a spork of oatmeal into her mouth. A lumpy paste without much taste, she halfway chewed the gruel and swallowed it with difficulty. She made a face and said, "Gross!" then turned to the apple juice.

The sweetness was welcome, but artificial. Only about a sip was to be had, as the small container was still frozen. She squeezed and shook it, but gave up, placing it back in its rightful resting place on the tray.

Squirting the jelly pack on to one half of one of the white bread pieces, it was palatable...but only because she was starving. Tess tried to remember..."What day is it? When had she actually eaten last?" taking notice of her growling stomach.

"It must have been lunch yesterday...Wednesday...today is Thursday....I was just brought in her last night." she reminded herself, promising to keep track of what day it was...no matter what!

"Bologna!" she announced to no one, having a eureka moment, remember her lunch at home...having treated herself to a bologna and Miracle Whip sandwich...a true Southern favorite...a blast from the past, from her youth that she craved out of the blue yesterday. She immediately regretted that being the last thing she had eaten and the only thing left in her stomach, and now this. Ugh!

She dutifully began peeling the hardboiled eggs, daintily adding the pepper and salt and made herself eat the eggs and remaining slice of bread...she had to keep up her strength.

With no clock and simply guessing, the only way Tess was able to know the hours passing was when another tray came around. Sitting on the bed she studied the remnants left on the breakfast tray now sitting on the floor next to the door.

Her thoughts turned to her home, to Evan, her life...How did she end up in this place? What was happening with her animals? Client calls? She had to get home! She had to use a phone!

She looked at the small stainless panel at the back of the wall above the bed. It contained a push button and small speaker area, so she knew it was some type of call button. She tentatively eyed it and then forced herself to just push it! She leaned in to it awaiting a reply that never came. After a minute or two, she pushed it again and this time heard a slight bussing coming from the hallway in intervals like a morse code.

She went to the door and anxiously waited, her face pressed to the small window trying to peer out. The arrival of a nurse from the unseen area to the left of the door came without warning and startled her to quickly take a step back.

"What do you want!" the woman demanded in a gruff, unfriendly tone, a permanent scowl across her face.

She reminded Tess of a Nurse Ratchett character with some type of sinister intent.

"Uh, I, I need to use a phone...I haven't been given a chance to use a phone and I need to call my attorney." she stammered like a scared child.

"I'll have to call a guard for that." she pronounced.

"I'd really appreciate it. I need to call..." the nurse was already walking away.

"Wait! Please wait!" Tess begged.
The nurse turned and returned to the window fiercely peering in at her.

"It is possible for me to get some aspirin?" Tess asked sweetly.

"What for?" the woman angrily protested.

"My head. It's been hurting really badly and I could really use some..."

"Just go lay down." the surly nurse ordered and returned to her station to answer a buzzing phone.

Tess stood there...pound, pound, pound! Her head throbbed like a beating drum.

The nurse and where she sat at the nurse's station were out of view, but she could hear her metamorphosis from surly and defiant to sweet and friendly, happily chatting on the phone.

She realized she would get nothing from her. She was seen as a criminal, not a human being. No one in here cared the slightest and here she was captive and at their mercy. Begrudgingly she took the nurse's advise and laid down trying to ease her mind and the throbbing pain. She had to call home and get the number for her attorney.

"What happened to being innocent until proven guilty? What happened to my right to a phone call? I haven't even been read my rights yet?" she was talking to herself again. This wasn't right!

Tess began to get angry, then scared, then upset. Shit! What could she do? Nothing. Absolutely nothing. She was stuck!

She closed her eyes, used her rag of a washcloth as an eye mask, the blackness now a welcome friend.

Voices mumbling, staff and officers coming in and out, walkie talkies burping and fizzing, telephone ringing...the morning activity of the medical ward of the detention center. She heard talk about prescriptions, blood pressure and various administrative items, all fragmented and floating around at random. Doors being unlocked then loudly banging shut. A few various male inmates shuffled by.

Tess would get up and try to see something, anything out that sliver of a window in her door, but defeated returned to the bunk again.

A wail came through the wall followed by rants and profanity. "My G. damned leg. I can't get up! I need a cane for my motherfucking leg!" a country sounding woman cursed.

"Help! Help! Nurse! Nurse! I need some fucking help! These G. damn people around here...they just don't fucking care! G. damn shitheads! I ain't just gonna..."
(slight pause)

"Nurse! Nurse! I need some fucking help! Please help me!" The voice sounding more desperate and manic. Some crazy older black woman, Tess identified by her drawl. Probably a meth or crackhead she guessed.

Funny how you can tell someone's ethnicity by their voice, she thought. In Cherokee County, black folk were rare. It was known from its history of white predominance, something Tess had been oblivious to when she moved here, oblivious because of the sheer beauty of the land.

She listened intently as a nurse finally came over to the room to the right of her and talked sweetly and condescendingly to the woman. "Now Mary, you need to settle down."

"I NEED some pain medication!" Mary screamed defiantly. "I hurt. I hurt real bad." she whimpered. "Your pills are coming soon with pill call. You need to go lay down and not cause such a fuss now." The nurse said sweetly.

Tess heard the sound of movement as if the crazy black woman was being helped back over to her bunk. With the thud of the closing door, it was quiet again, but only for a few minutes.

Mary was back at it again...cussing and conversing...talking and shouting all kinds of random tirades. Then she broke out in song, a solemn hymn that she serenaded herself to sleep.

Laying there staring up at the ceiling, Tess wondered about Mary, if she might end up her cellmate? "Now that's a scary thought!" she murmured, now more glad for this private room. But why was she here in the jail's psycho ward...and why wouldn't they let her use the phone?

A lovely lunch of a Bologna sandwich with one pack of mustard, one small bag of chips and jello was brought in and her breakfast tray collected. Her new "friend," the inmate orderly smiled his snaggle tooth grin at her with those eager eyes.

She thanked him politely for the tray and asked his escorting officer about using the phone. "They'll come get you." he assured and so she waited, meekly eating the sandwich like a little mouse hunched over, sitting cross-legged on the bunk, holding the limp bread in both hands, wishing for a miracle and some Miracle Whip!

No Talking!
She didn't hear a peep out of her distraught neighbor, Mary. She must be sleeping she thought.

She heard charts held in door holders being slid out and flipped through. Female nurse voices discussed medications, got doctor's names, called in prescriptions, and administered pills as assigned.

She heard the low rumbling of a man's voice, like a subdued grizzly bear just being woken up from hibernation. The sound of a nearby door open and a nurse conversing with that someone with a very low voice. Through the metal door she strained to make out what they were saying. The more she listened, the more she recognized the voice. It was Brian. He was right next door!

The nurse sounded concerned about his blood pressure and it was the topic of discussion along with a long list of medications and doctor's names. Tess pressed her face against the glass trying to see but could only make out the side of a friendly looking blonde nurse with glasses...a definite improvement from the witch of a woman from the fourth shift last night.

She sat back on the bunk...now her up and down from the window of the door and back routine was firmly established. More voices and the nurse sounded like she was at her door now! Tess thought she would enter but instead heard and exchange between the nurse and a colleague.

"Why is this inmate in here?" she asked

"Which one"

"Sanderson" ...obviously not seeing anything in her chart or file or whatever paperwork was there.

"Security risk." was the reply and they moved on to Mary's room, greeted with sobs and baby talk like that of a little child. Mary got her "medicine" probably Methadone and was put back to bed.

Security risk? What in the world was that all about? Tess was reeling. She needed to use the phone and call someone. She tried the call button several more times and each time was promised that someone would come to get her so she could use the phone. Waiting and waiting, not able to gage how much time had passed, she tried not to panic. Definitely an exercise in patience.

Damn! She didn't want to end up like Mary...some raving lunatic reduced to groveling and sniveling, but she was getting really close to it...teetering on the brink. "God, this is a nightmare." she confirmed to herself.

"Why won't the let me use the phone? Why are they holding me in here? It just doesn't make sense!" she told herself.

Then she got it! "They're holding me here so I *can't* call anybody!"

"Shit! Shit! Damn! I wan't my Mommy!" she whined hugging her knees and rocking to and fro like a patient from Girl Interrupted. She wanted to start yelling and carrying on like Mary had. She wanted to start screaming of the injustice being done to her, but she couldn't utter a sound. She had no voice.

She amused herself by thinking back over the last 24 hours and the parallels she had seen with television and movies and her predicament she now found herself in. It had all happened so fast and within hours she had been plucked out of her beautiful life and given a starring role in "Girls Gone Bad!"

She kept thinking the cliche' that it was all just a bad dream and she would wake up back on the farm, with Evan, the dogs all snuggled on their oh so comfortable bed. But it was all starting to sink in now. Maybe her life as she knew it was never going to be the same again.

"Oh God," she prayed, "please help me get out of here. Oh God, please help me."

Even with the earnest and desperate prayer, she felt like some how God was mocking her. Flashbacks of her life and anything remotely unChristian she'd ever done zooming in at her. She saw herself like Jesus...getting her back whipped with a cat of nine tails, being persecuted, carrying a cross, falling down to her knees, exhausted, bloody.

She saw Jesus walking beside her with his cross, but it was being carried by a couple of his disciples as Jesus casually strolled along smoking a big fat joint, small trickles of blood of no consequence from his thorny crown. He smiled lovingly at her, exhaling a big puff of smoke, then he turned into Evan and sprouted angel wings and flew away!

Another 18 Hours
The day turned into night and she was still not given a phone call. A fitful sleep coupled with the stress of not knowing what was happening on the outside and the rock solid bed kept her up and down throughout the night.

Her head was STILL throbbing and STILL no aspirin.

Mary had an outburst whenever she regained consciousness and at one point between f-words started singing a hymn that was actually very soothing and helped Tess doze off for a minute. Her door opened with a bang that jolted her upright, the officer at her door was a haze coming into focus. It looked like the same one who had brought her here originally, Ms. Officer Androgenous.

"Ok, Sanderson. You're going to the Pod." she announced. "Get your stuff."

"Okey dokey." Tess blurted out and regretted it immediately. She was such a good-girl dork. She hoped the officer didn't think she was mocking her in some way.

With her bin packed and mat folded on top, she was directed down the nondescript corridors..."Turn left here. Stop, stand here. Through this door. Go right. Through that door. Stay to the right. Stay by the wall." They had a lively conversation.

Buzzing into the still and shadowy Pod, the door opened to the open area and Tess anticipated now who or what would be her cellmate/roommate. Mary was still in "medical" so she wouldn't have to worry about her. But...

"Room 3" she directed and Tess was led into a 2-bunk room which held two sleeping inmates...one snoring softy, both curled up under the orange cotton blankets with their backs to them, facing the rear wall of the cell. They did not wake.

"Put your pad on the floor." she motioned to the empty left wall across from the toilet, desk and shelf. Tess gingerly put down her things trying to be quiet, the officer exiting, closing the door carelessly with a bang with no regard for the sleeping "guests."

The woman on the lower bunk turned and looked out from under her blanket, hazy and disoriented.

"Sorry to disturb you." Tess apologized in a whisper. "That's ok Baby." the woman said softly. "They don't care what time it is around here. What time do that clock say out there?" she motioned.

Tess stepped up to her familiar place...the small window in the door...and pressed her face to it.

She scanned the room with the other rooms across the open area numbered 9-16. Another set above with a balcony and catwalk. The stainless dining tables in the center empty.

To the right she saw the guard's desk sitting in the middle towards the offset exit/entry door. Above the door she spied a large clock. It struck her now as being a friendly face...like a long-lost friend you find unexpectedly in a crowded room. After not knowing the time for the last, what 24 hours or more, it was a welcome relief.

"It's 4:30" she whispered, her roommate already back to sleep.

Welcome to J-Pod!
The fluorescent light above clicked and then beamed at full power flooding the small cell with bright light. The voltage increase produced a buzzing like some huge bumble bee hovering above in the center of the room. The light was a blinding wake-up call...the jail's version of your very own personal sunrise, with the automatic door locking mechanisms whirring and releasing like dominos falling down the row of doors.

Tess sat up and looked at the door. The women on the bunks moved slowly with grunts and moans. "It's too early for this." the woman on the lower bunk said, reaching for a pair of glasses on a left-over space above her head with her bible and a few other paperbacks neatly stacked.

She was a fair skinned black woman with short, cropped hair, a refined nose, full lips and a model's cheek bones. Although Tess figured her to be around her age, or maybe a little older, she could tell that probably under different circumstances and with cosmetics, she could still pull off 30-something easily.

The woman studied Tess for a second then swung her legs to the floor. She wore a set of long johns and white socks and had a brown piece of fabric as a head band.

"Hi, I'm Staci." she said. "Is this your first time in jail?" she instinctively asked, knowing full well the answer.

"Yes." Tess confirmed.

Staci reached to the hooks under the small shelf, grasping a bin's flat top which acted as a hanger for her uniform top. "I'm just going to have to wear it wet." she said. "I washed it last night and it's still not dry."

Tess now noticed a trash can with soapy water and whites still soaking in it below the shelf, a small puddle creeping from it under the edge of the sink lingering its way to Tess's bed mat on the floor. Staci was slim and looked in shape, her top half resembling a gymnast or a runner, the lower more typical of her genes with full legs and backside that would give JLo or Beyonce a run for their money. She shimmied the damp garment on over her thermal top and quickly pulled on her canvas pants over the thermal leggings.

"It's hard to get these things to dry in here when it's been raining on the outside." she said.
"It rained today?" Tess asked, reminded of how oblivious and isolated she had been for the last 24-48 hours.

"It rained yesterday." Staci confirmed.

A loud female voice called out from outside the rooms, echoing in the large hall. "Ladies, it's time to get up! It's time for breakfast. Come out of your rooms with your hands up with your cup and your spork!"

"Trays are on the floor! Trays are on the floor!"

Staci slapped the rear end of the other roommate, jutting out over the edge as she lay lifeless on her side.

"Sissy! Get up girl. Breakfast." Staci chided.

Sissy groaned and sat straight up, her long black cornrowed braids flowing around her face and down her back. A sea of tiny serpent weaves, braided into one large tri-mix. She was a deep dark chocolate and a direct contrast to Staci's coffee with cream light hue.

The whites of Sissy's eyes shown bright as the rest of her became part of the shadow in the corner of the top bunk. She rubbed her eyes and squinted.

"Who you?" she asked looking at Tess.

Sissy smiled her fang-like grin, her top front teeth missing between her canines. She quickly put her hand in front of her mouth and said "Hi" through her fingers.

"Well at least that bitch ain't here this mornin' makin' us take showers." Sissy grumbled in her soft little voice as she made her way down the desktop and stool serving as her steps.

Tess stood off to the side as Sissy dressed for breakfast, putting her uniform on over her thermals as Staci had done. She wondered why she had no socks, underwear or bra or even a t-shirt, and they did, obvious from the laundry they had hanging all around the room.

Naked underneath the top and bottom canvas ensemble and in plastic slip on sandals, she was cold and shivered as she waited.

"Be sure to make your bed up now!" Sissy sang as she pulled hers together by standing on the stool and reaching up and over.

"Yeah, that's right." Staci added, "You always got to make your bed up every time they let us out...and don't forget your cup and spork."

The three new roommates made their way out through their unlocked door and stood outside against the wall beside. Tess followed their lead.

They faced other women across the room who looked tired, disheveled and some just plain worn out and faded. "Rode hard and put up wet." as the saying goes, all dutifully holding their small cups.

A white female officer stood before them at the head of the room to their right in the open area between the tables and a drink station of sorts with a sink and a fountain like machine and small microwave. A large hot liquid dispenser was also on the utility counter with another faucet beside it.

Tess's eyes scanned across the back of the room and up to her trusty clock...7:10 it read, the brightness of the lights sending glares off the stainless tables.

"Good morning ladies!" the guard greeted them. "If everyone who is going to eat is out of your room, please secure your doors.

Thump! Thump! Thump! Thump! as all doors were pushed securely shut from their open-out positions. Staci with a quick butt from her fabulous rump closed theirs in one swift bend.

"Up comes down and down goes up." the officer ordered.

A line of women from upstairs began filing around the top perimeter and down the side stairway towards a metal cart piled high with plastic trays.

"Go up." Staci told her and she followed two women to her right up the other set of stairs on their side going to the upper level.

She didn't immediately get it, but watched as the women filed up and then around and down like a trail of ants marching towards the picnic their scout had informed them about.

"Oh-e-oh. E-oh-oh!" she mused as she envisioned all the women marching and chanting like the Seven Dwarfs, fully expecting them to break into song and do a dance routine all over the catwalk and down the stairs, basking in the glowing fluorescent spotlights.

A slight smile crossed her face at the thought of everyone dancing and singing, racing around, jumping on the tops of the tables, kicking off the sandals and sliding across the floor in their stocking feet. Waltzing the guards around like some new Mel Brook's jailhouse musical.

Tess and her roommates were standing now on the top level directly across from their room. She abruptly came back to realty, bumping into a woman in front of her who had stopped. A large round woman with grown out bleach blonde hair, the black roots some 2-3 inches long, turned and called out in a whisper, lisping "Hey! Watch out!" her mouth void of any teeth.

Tess wasn't sure if she was more surprised by bumping into the woman or the fact that the poor thing was so homely, with teeth or without. Her gums showed off as her upper lip curled at her snarl.

"Oh, oh! I'm so sorry." Tess whispered, touching her arm. The woman grunted and turned around. The women stood single file waiting to get their trays. They inched along murmuring amongst themselves. Around the top balcony and step by step down the stairs, each woman handed a tray and milk carton and then scattered haphazardly like marbles to their respective tables and preferred seating arrangements.

Tess took her tray from the guard who she noticed had a smooth complexion and a pretty face. She wore rubber gloves as she quickly, robotically handed out some 60+ trays.

Tess made her way slowly toward and open spot at the nearest table, but was quickly rebuffed by a young, tomboy of a black girl with short dread-like braids sticking out in all directions.

"That seat's saved!" she said in an unusually low voice, but non-threatening.

"Oh!" Tess replied, somewhat surprised.

She looked around for Staci and Sissy but they were already at a table that was now full. She got a sudden and strange bout of anxiety from grade school lunchroom politics past and cautiously approached the next table and its resident eaterati.

A woman probably her age, but looked 10 years older...with big black bushy eyebrows and grey streaks framing her face and running intermittently through her tousled hair pulled into a bobby-sox level pony tail...smiled at her with her mouth closed and said in a friendly tone, "You can sit here." Tess welcomed the invitation, sat and watched with interest as her table filled with eight others.

"Hi, I'm Pam."

"Hi. Tess." they introduced themselves.

She looked down at her tray to assess corn flakes and a big square biscuit with some type of brown gravy with the consistency of jelly slopped on top. There was also a small serving of scrambled eggs...the only thing really that appealed to her.

The small salt and pepper packets and one packet of sugar completed the breakfast offerings.

Tess noticed a heavy-set woman with straight stringy hair up the table from her quickly place a sugar packet in her breast pocket. At the head of the table sat a woman? She had a youthful, Howdy-Dudy of a face, round cheeks, with a half inch of dark stubble creating a 4-oclock shadow on her skull. She ate with her elbows out and happily talked to her friend not giving a second thought to the food she was exposing in her mouth.

Tess peppered her eggs and squeezed the excess water from them by pressing with her spork. In two sporks they were finished.

Being lactose intolerant she passed on the cereal and looked at the "thing" with gravy on it with dread and doubt.

"You want your cereal?" the dike asked, pulling Tess out of her face-off with the gravy blob taunting her growling stomach to "eat me."

"Uh, no. You can have it." she offered.

Before the words were fully out of her mouth, her tray was scooped up and the cereal shoveled off onto another.

"You want your biscuit?" the large woman with stringy hair asked, her eyes hungry.

"Uh, no. Go ahead." and her other new "friend" scooped it off too!

"God, they are like starving." she thought to herself. Pam leaned over intimately, her eyes twinkling,

"They'll eat anything." she whispered, gumming the cereal the best she could.

The room humming with conversation was quickly "shooshed" and "shooshed" a second and third time as the officer stood at the head of the room waiting for quiet.

"Ok Ladies! Bring it down!" she called out, holding her arms out to the side and motioning downward.

"Bring it down! Quiet please." she stood tapping her foot, panning back and forth, her hands now clasped behind her back.

Once she had full quiet and attention, she began pacing methodically back and forth.

"Many of you know me, but for those of you who are new to J-Pod, my name is Deputy Preston or Miss Preston. I run an orderly Pod and have rules. If you don't know the rules or have a question about my rules, ask someone."

"Firstly, my desk...if I'm not at my desk, you do not touch anything on my desk. If anyone takes anything off my desk, you will be locked down!"

She was firm and direct and obviously meant business. All eyes were on her and followed as her pacing now took her around the perimeter of the tables.

"There is to be a three-foot radius around my desk at all times. If I have another officer at my desk, the nurse or any other personnel at my desk, do not approach me. You will wait until I am finished. Understood?"

"Yes Miss Preston." the group of women, now reduced to preschoolers, answered in unison.
"I treat you with respect, if you treat me with respect." she continued.

Pam said under her breath, "Here it comes...here it comes." in her funny drawl.

Officer Preston circled the tables with a hint of a grin trying to break through her straight face and Tess thought she could see she was trying to fight it and waiting for "Miss Preston" to bust out laughing any minute.

"Ok, Miss Preston! We're ready!" a raspy voice jeered good naturedly from her captive audience.

Preston smirked again. "And, if you don't like how I run my Pod, I suggest you either... stay in your room or bond out!" many of the women shouting out the directive with her.

"If you're done with your food, return your trays and go back to your rooms."

And with that, everyone began shuffling around, taking trays back to the cart, heating water in the microwave, getting more of the liquid they so disarmingly call coffee.

TGIF!

In her room, she sat on her bed pad on the floor. Sissy stood at the sink preening in the mirror plate and Staci on her bunk.

"She'll let us out for free time after the cleaners get through. It should only be a few minutes." she informed Tess matter-of-factly.

"I really need to use the phone. I haven't been given the chance to call anybody and I've been here since Wednesday night. What day is it?" she asked.

"It's Friday morning, baby." Staci said sweetly. "I'll help you get to the phone." she reassured with a smile.

The doors buzzed open and Miss Preston yelled, "Ok Ladies, it's free time!"

Staci launched toward the door and urged Tess to "get to the phones!" pushing to get out but it was still locked. She rattled it back and forth and it a few seconds it was open.

"Don't let it shut behind you!" she warned as Tess gently set the door so it wouldn't close all the way.

She walked quickly to the bank of (four) phones...for over 60 women...and asked a young girl standing behind another who was already on the phone if she was in line.

"I'm after her and she's after me," she said pointing to another women sitting at the table closest to the phones.

"Is anyone in line after you for the phone?" Tess asked her.

"Nope! I guess you are!" she laughed as Tess sat down beside her to wait.

"So what are you in here for?" asked the jovial woman, seeming as if she were trying to make conversation versus just being nosey.

"Oh, it's a big misunderstanding." Tess sheepishly said, provoking a big laugh from her now newest best friend.

"Yeah, yeah...that's what they all say." she retorted with a big smile, touching her arm.

"I'm innocent! I'm innocent!" she joked holding her hands up and waving them in the air.

"No. I really am." Tess protested. "Really!" She laughed at the woman's fun spirit which was infectious and spreading.

"Yeah, yeah...me too!" she said with that big, perfect smile.

Tess was relieved to see someone who still had their teeth and liked this woman immediately, even though she was giving her a little bit of a hard time.

She noticed the deep laugh lines around her sparkling eyes, knowing they were chiseled in over decades of laughs, reminders of all those good times. She had a kind of country face...whatever that means...to be best described a plain but attractive with traits likely passed down through generations, way back to the country's earliest settlers. "She probably looks just like her grandmother and great grandmother and great, great grandmother." Tess thought.

"I'm Denny." she said.

"Tess"

"Nice to meet you!" and they nodded at each other exchanging the greeting.

"I've been trying to get in touch with my Mom and I can't get through." Denny complained, frustrated.

"I was just moved over here and she doesn't even know where I am....she'll go to visitation in Forsyth and I won't be there. I guess she'll find out then." she rattled off.

Denny was on the verge of manic. Probably hyper naturally, but Tess gathered this was a natural state given the circumstances and the adrenaline that came with the situation.

"What about you?" Tess asked.

"What about me?" Denny countered back.

"Why are you in here?" Tess chuckled.
Denny laughed too as she turned towards her, leaning in like she was going to tell her this big secret.

"Drugs, Man! Drinking and drugs."

She was happy to explain her situation and told Tess she had been in the neighboring county on a probation violation, but had gotten in some trouble in Cherokee, so was sent here.

She had been "clean," working and doing good until some sort of (blubbering) mishap had put her back into the system. Tess tried to follow what she was detailing, but it was hard to do.

"My Mom's 60 years old. I can't keep putting her through this." Denny lamented.

"Her damn home phone won't accept calls from here. I've been trying to call her cell phone, but she doesn't even turn it on!"

"You'd think with me being in JAIL she'd keep her dang cell phone on...but NOOOOOO! Oh no! Not my dear sweet wonderful mother...bless her heart!" Denny complained.

Tess was amused and laughed a little more. Denny was almost cartoon-like with her exaggerated expressions and enthusiasm.

"I'm sure she really cares about you and wants to hear from you." Tess tried to reassure her.

"Yes, she does...she really does." Denny whispered, her tone totally changing.

"She's been taking care of my girls for me. She's always been there for me. I've got to get off the dope this time and do right. I think I can make it this time, I really do." She started getting choked up. It was odd the connection and compassion Tess felt for Denny in just a few minutes.

A funny, charming, personable woman, with a long-term dependency problem...a drug addict in hiding, in plain sight. Tess would not have guessed if Denny hadn't told her. She must be so naive.

"Dove! Denny Dove! Phone!" someone called out and her face lit up and her eyebrows raised and she quickly jumped from the stool over to the bay of phones. Maybe she would get through this time.

Tess almost started crying when she thought of her own mother. 80 years young. Her best friend. What worry she must be under. How much could her heart take? She hoped it wasn't too much for her. God! If her mother got ill from this blunder, she could not live. Evan's dumb mistake in judgement. Hers too, for enabling him, unknowingly going along with whatever he was doing. Ahhh! So frustrating. She hoped her Mom was ok. She had to get word to her that she was!

Tess looked around at all the women sitting at the tables chatting, getting a bright red kool-aid from the dispenser up front, microwaving popcorn...the smell moving like a dense, slow cloud, permeating the space with its buttery and burnt aroma.

Young, old, all different shapes and sizes, even dressed alike, they each held their originality. Mostly a Caucasian group, Tess did the math and figured 10% were Black, 3% Hispanic and probably 80% on meth, judging from the snaggle-toothed grins or gums flashing as the women talked and laughed. Scanning the other inmates she sat and waited.

"Wow, a full-fledged Mullett!" she thought to herself, noticing a small, petite woman with cute features and big blue eyes. Her light brown hair stood spiking straight up, like a crown from behind her ears to her forehead. The back was straight and long, past her shoulders, a total 1980s throw-back.

The woman was sitting engrossed in coloring with crayons some kindergarten image of a cat, her right hand going back and forth like crazy, her eyes staring, deranged at her art.

She saw her roommate Staci cutting up with another black woman as she stood braiding another light-skinned Mulatto's bleach-blonde hair, sitting patiently as she was preened over.

The younger of the three had a very pretty, round face. Only until she rose from her seat did Tess notice her to be VERY pregnant.

She wondered why such an innocent looking young woman, mother-to-be, was in jail? It struck her as odd. The whole thing was completely surreal and seemed off.

Several women walked around the Pod perimeter getting their morning exercise. One of the two televisions dangling above was on and showing the morning news with the volume turned down, sub-titles taking up the bottom quarter of the screen.

Tess couldn't make out the words from her vantage point and only recognized the familiar face of her favorite local news anchor, Brenda Wood. Then it struck her. What if they had been on the news? She had seen busts on the news with late-night seizures of a meth lab at a mobile home park somewhere in the foothills of the North Georgia Mountains, the officer proudly stating how much the seizure yielded, how much it was worth on the street and then followed by the infamous mug shots of all those brought in on the sting.

"Oh, those poor fools." she thought, caught in the drag net, looking sullen, disheveled and dull. She thought how stupid these people were...the lowly low of their society. Trailer trash, ex-cons or worse, feeding off dumb kids who should know better, addicts and the working poor looking for some sort of relief, albeit misguided, to their sad, tragic lives.

She couldn't understand the attraction of meth...some wild concoction of cold medicine, pseudoephedrine, bleach, embalming fluid, and whatever else could be thrown in (she had heard tales of).

Tess remembered another story on the news about a couple purchasing large quantities of these items, particularly the cold medicine, at their neighborhood Wal-mart, with an off-duty police officer behind them in line. They were followed home, to the trailer park, where in their little box of a home was to be meth lab, and were caught in the act.

She also read a Newsweek article about the Meth Epidemic sweeping the nation and the far-reaching effect it has had on our working-poor and up. From medical care, emergency room visits (up over 200% in Atlanta), child welfare services, over-crowding in jails, a stark increase in admittance to burn units from related explosions, all with the nation's tax-base footing the bill.

The article also documented a rise in crimes due to Meth of Domestic Violence up 62%; Assault up 53%; Burglary up 70%; and I.D. theft up 27%. A 40% rise in children taken from homes due to methamphetamine use; and 58% of County police citing Meth as their biggest problem.

Tess intently watched the news images flash across the screen, horrified at the thought that her picture, alongside Evan, Brian and Diana's might make the evening news under the headline of "300 Marijuana Plants Seized! Local Realtor Implicated."

The tragic thought of mug shots and the news of the grow house was blown to shreds as her mind wandered to an image of her coming down the courthouse steps in large Jackie-O sunglasses, hounded by reporters, her hand trying to block the paparazzi's cameras.

"No comment! No comment! Other than I'm innocent!"

"Innocent. Innocent." she whispered to herself.

"Hey, Little Miss Innocent!" Denny called to her, as if reading her mind.

"Phone!"

She sprang up and took a few running steps to reach the waiting phone.

Life Lines

"How do these work?" she asked Denny, still with that permanent big grin on her face.

"You dial 1 and then 0, then the number. It's a collect call and you get 15 minutes."

Tess sat down on the stool looking at the keypad in front of her. Her mind went blank. She struggled to remember any phone numbers. Somehow she remembered her home number, her cell and her sister's number.

She tried her home landline. It rang and rang. She was relieved when Frank answered.

He detailed the remnants of the search. Her computer had been confiscated and some of Evan's things...incriminating enough to get her here...from his pile on his side of the bed. Frank's little pipe and some seeds. That was all he knew of that had been taken.

The house, especially her office, had been torn apart with papers and receipts thrown all over the place like confetti.

The dogs were fine. The horses were fine. Hang tight and they and Attorney Billy were going to get her out.

"We've got your cell phone here." he informed. This was good news and something she didn't quite understand why or how it happened, but it didn't matter...at least her clients could call. DeeDee could answer.

Evan had already called...the day before. He said not to worry. He loves you and he's going to do whatever it takes to get you out of this." Frank reported. "You shouldn't be in there."

She clung to the words. "He's already talked to his mother about getting you a property bond."

"But there is no bond." she cried.

"We're working on that." Frank assured her, sounding very confident and in the know.

He let her know all he knew so far and kindly reported that, no, it had not been on the Atlanta news! He detailed the latest developments he had learned of...more people Evan knew that had been investigated. Every friend, every client, every worker in the remodeling company was under scrutiny. He had obviously been followed for some time.

Frank mentioned several familiar names that had also been arrested in association with the sting but had bonded out and not been charged.

"I don't get it Frank. How can they charge me with 'possession of over 10 pounds of marijuana' when I had none? How can they charge me with 'trafficking' when I was doing no such thing?" Tess asked.

"Listen, it won't hold up. They're trying to stick it to you because you are the girlfriend. Hang in there. Billy is coming to see you today or tomorrow."

The automated operator warned that their time was running short so they said their good-byes, Tess calling out "I'll call back later. Give Evan my love when he calls!"

She hung up the phone slowly, as Staci poked her head around the divider. "Did you get in touch with anyone, Baby?" she asked with what seemed like real concern.

"Yes, my house. My lawyer is supposed to be coming to see me today or tomorrow."

"Oh, that soon?" Staci sounded impressed.

"We have free time until 10:15" she let her know as she quickly straddled the attached seat and punched in the numbers, settling in.

Just like clockwork, Miss Preston called "lock down" at 10:15, the women scattering to finish heating things in the microwave and getting scolded. Those on the phones anxiously saying their good-byes, trying desperately to hold on to each second before hanging up. The other's taking their sweet time slowing shuffling in all directions to their respective rooms and up each set of stairs.

The three women were back in Room 3 and Tess sat cross-legged on her bed pad as Sissy climbed up to her perch on the top bunk. "Shoot! I didn't even get to call my Mama or my sister." she whined, settling into place and opening a large paperback book. Tess noticed the cover, Lasher by Anne Rice.

She looked at Sissy, now reading, with her exotic dark skin, long braids, flashing almond eyes, and her own natural fangs. She thought it fitting. She was a beautiful garish vampire herself...locked in her cell, just doing her time until she could get out and start bloodsucking again! Tess imagined, entertaining herself.

Staci was preening in the mirror plate, fussing over her hair, a short afro.

"It's just getting too long." she complained. "I look like some kind of sponge head." Sissy giggled and her childlike tone made Tess giggle too. Sissy automatically covered her mouth.

"So what they git you for Tess?" Staci asked, still looking at herself and running a comb through her short springs of hair.

"Oh gosh. My boyfriend was allegedly involved in growing marijuana, and they think I'm in on it." she explained.

"Well, was you?" Sissy asked now giving her full attention. Staci did too.

Tess did a doubletake between the two and exclaimed, "Heck no!"

"Hell no, Baby. Never admit anything. You got that right." Staci advised going back to her hair.

"No, really. I didn't. IF he was involved, he purposely kept it from me. I didn't know anything about some house growing pot...I...I"

"You really didn't know?" Staci questioned, spinning around for face her, looking down her nose through a pair of tiny wire rimmed glasses, her hand on her hip.

"No, I didn't." Tess said firmly, staring back at her.

Staci stood sizing up the situation for a moment, their eyes still locked.

She took off her glasses, shifted her weight to the other hip and declared, "Well, alright then. You shouldn't have anything to worry about." accepting Tess's truth.

Staci regrouped and began her cross examination, pacing back and forth about five steps each way on the small open piece of floor.

She said, "Oh Baby, that's no good." when Tess told her of the actual charges and no bond. "Tsk, tsk, tsk" and shook her head.

"You got a good attorney, don't you?" she asked.

"He came highly recommended, but I've never needed an attorney before." Tess answered.

"And you ain't never been in jail before?"

"No."

"Never been arrested before?"

"No."

"Never been on probation?"

"No. Nothing. I've never even had a traffic ticket!"

"Well, you'll be alright 'den. You ain't got nothin' to worry about. You can plead First Offenders and probably only get probation." Staci tried to reassure her.

"Probation! I didn't do anything. I need the charges dropped. I could lose my real estate license." Tess exclaimed.

"You do real estate?" Staci smiled. "I've got a friend you need to talk to who wants to sell his house."

J-Pod: Lunch
They talked while Sissy read and by lunch at 12:15 Tess had learned that Staci was a career criminal...the last 20 years of her 40-something life spent in and out of jail and prison time before this.

Staci's game was fraud...bad checks, identity theft. She confessed to having champagne tastes and not a budget to match. Her first husband was a player and took the sweet, young, impressionable thang from a strict, good-girl household to a life of cons and the next big take.

"You know, I had it going on before I got with Antonio. Never been in trouble, had good credit, a good job and a future. I was going to go to school." Staci lamented.

"I hadn't never been with no man before him and he wouldn't let up...he had to have me. I was with him for 15 years! Who knows what my life would have been if I'd got to school and not gotten pregnant and married Antonio."

"He hit me one too many times. I was so tired of his shit, and that was it. I left him." Staci confessed.

"Amen!" Sissy chimed in, looking up from her book.

"I've got a son and a daughter and I'm a grandmother. I just got to get out of here. The sooner the better!"

"When will you be getting out?" Tess asked, concerned.

"I've got to get a court date next week, so hopefully soon." Staci hoped. Tess nodded.

"So tell me about the con, Staci?" Tess asked, curious. "How do you pull it off?"

An evil grinch-like grin crossed Staci's face and her eyes sparkled. She sat on the desk stool backwards, facing Tess, her hands on her knees. She licked her lips and pushed herself up, straightening her arms, elbows locked.

"Ok...you really want to know this?" she asked, gearing up.

"Yes! For my own protection!" Tess laughed. "But, joking aside, I find you fascinating!"

"You aren't going to use any of this against me, are you?" Staci asked and let out a big "Ha!" and began to begin again, taking a big breath.

"With the checks, what we'd do is get some out of the mail...somebody's mail when they were sending bills out. We get their check and get the routing and account numbers off of it. 'den we order us some checks...you know the kind you get the order forms from magazines or the Sunday paper...with the designs on them. And we have a fake i.d. made up that matched the check name and address on it."

"Where would you write the checks? Would you buy merchandise or cash them" Tess asked, very intrigued.

"We'd take them up to the casino in NC on the reservation. They cash them at the cashier for up to $2500. Just like that!"

"And with the credit card scam...my boyfriend at the time...he was into all this...knew the guy with the fake i.d.s and all that. He stole a briefcase from a car lot that had a bunch of credit applications in it. We went to Kinko's and used their computer, you know, by the hour...had the social security numbers, pulled credit reports. Got I.D.s made and went into Home Depot and Lowe's...places like that...Circuit City and opened accounts. It was so easy. We got all kinds of stuff and had these big credit lines. I mean, we knew what these people had already from their credit reports, so it jived together."

"Wow!" Tess said. "That's pretty amazing."

"Well, not really." Staci rebuffed.

"We got receipts with credit card numbers on them from rental car companies too. They just throw that shit in the trash for anybody to get."

Tess nodded. "Well, gosh, it sure seems like you really put a whole lot of time and effort into it. I mean, you are such a personable lady with a lot going for her. If you put that much into something legit, who knows where you'd be today instead of here!" ...

"You got that right!" Staci declared standing up.

"Damn sure not in here!" and she and Sissy high-fived laughing.

"I tell you what Miss T. (Tess's new nickname) I'm done. I got my grandchildren, my children...my dad's in the hospital for lung cancer, dying and I can't be there...I'm stuck in this damn place!" Staci testified.

"I'm done, I tell you. This is it for me and I'm in here for something I didn't even do!"

"Yeah, that's what we all say, right?" Tess joked.

Staci looked at her sternly for a second, lips pursed and her hand on her hip...then smiled her big grin..."Baby, you got that right!"

Frank, Dee and Fam to the Rescue
Lunchtime came and went with the same drill as breakfast. Tess jockeyed for the phone again..."I'm after you." "Who's after you?" and standing or sitting on the nearest stool to wait.

She called her sister out-of-state and got her at home unexpectedly. It was worth trying since it was one of the only numbers she remembered...other than her home land line and her cell.

"Laura, hi, it's me." Tess whimpered.

"Oh, I heard what happened. Frank called Mom and then me. It's so terrible! I'm so sorry this happened." she consoled.

"How is Mom?"

"Well, of course she's worried about you, but she's trying to stay calm."

"Tell her I'm ok. I just need to get a bond and get back home. With all these bills from the renovation projects, payments behind, the horses, the dogs, the farm...everything...I'm so worried. And the attorney. I need to get him on retainer so I can get out of here and keep working!"

"We'll get that taken care of." her loving sister reassured her.

"He's supposed to be coming to see you and Frank and Dee are taking care of things at the farm. You just sit tight. You've got things working for you and the whole family supports you!" Laura said lovingly.

Tears welled up. Tess was so thankful to have such a wonderful supportive family. The motto gleaned from her Grandfather had been, "There is no test to a man's character better than how he reacts when confronted with adversity." Something like that!

It was a relief and lifted a weight off her to a degree. She was amused by the "whole family" comment as her immediate family was small, with just her mother, sister, three aunties and a dozen adult 1st cousins dotted around the United States.

Her Aunties were her mother's sisters, now all seniors in their 80s, who had been there and done that throughout their lives. But Tess didn't think they ever had a child (or Niece!) incarcerated before, or at least she never heard of any such scandal within the family. She had the accolade of being the first...the one and only! She was all too embarrassed by the stupidity of it all. Having time to reassess much of what had led to this.

Tess had good relations with her Aunts. Probably because their mother was like her own. The family had always been matriarchal, her grandmother raised her, after coming to help her mother transition after a divorce, with two young daughters.

The temporary situation lasted some 30 years and her beloved Mommy2 (second Mom), passing away at the ripe age of 93.

Tess's mom had cared for her to the end and then did the same for her stepfather, Roe, a former tough as nails Military Man, retired Army Major, who served in World War II, Korea and Vietnam. Roe lived to tell about it, unlike most of the men in his EOD Hazardous Devices Bomb Squad Unit.
Roe had a heart of gold and a ho-ho-ho chuckle that he was able to capitalize on when in retirement he went on to play Santa Claus at the local Mall 5 years running.

He joked and laughed all the time and was one heck of a fellow. A rebellious teen, Tess had kept him on his toes, but the battle was short and sweet with Major Roe driving his forces through to safe territory. He kept her on the straight and narrow and instilled a sense of pride of accomplishment and let her desire to please and make her family proud shine.

To her mother and grandmother, she was a darling who could be anything, do anything and they were her staunchest advocates. To Roe, she was his top cadet who he could send to battle in this world and hoped she would not return wounded with a broken heart. He loved her in his own way and she his...of this they were both certain.

Tess's sister was 6 years her senior and had been off to college when their mother married Roe. They had settled in the military town in NC, near the big army base and Tess's mother had met Roe through her work.

They were friends only, with Roe being sent back home to his family in Alabama with strict orders not to try to pursue their friendship any further once Tess's Mom was informed of his wife and boys. Even though it wasn't a happy family and Roe was not a happy man in it, he was resigned to his fate and would do the right thing and return home...he himself wounded with a crack in his heart...to care for an ill-tempered and ailing spouse and kids who disrespected him due to a history of drinking.

There are many days in history that our parents lived through and always remember, particularly those in the military. D-Day, Pearl Harbor, Normandie. And, to Baby Boomer's or Gen X or Y'rs, there aren't that many dates that stick out other than the assasination of JFK, MLK and John Lennon or Kurt Cobain's untimely death.

But to Tess, the day that truly changed her life (other than the day she was arrested!) was the day some 10 years after he was dutifully sent back to Alabama when Roe called. At her mother's "hello", she was greeted with the words, "We buried her today."

At first, she didn't know who the morbid caller was, caught off-guard. But it was Roe, now free to pursue the life he had wanted...the life with her.

Tess had a pretty middle-class childhood and the addition of Roe was an upheaval at first, with no man in the household ever her entire first 13 years. Her grandmother stayed on and Tess spent her junior and senior high years with three parental units keeping watch and giving kudos to her good grades, and acceleration in work-study program, starting work at 16 at the Winn Dixie as a cashier, then upgrading to retail to the local Mall.

When it came time for college, she wa' go...not because of any lack of love f grandmother, mother or step-father, bu. get out on her own. She moved to Atlanta to school. Not too far from N.C., but not too close either. Her sister had stayed at the picturesque college town in NC, her alma matter and went on to become a staff member there.

Laura was a true flowerchild in every sense of the word having come of age in the 1970s. She was a free spirit that had gotten grounded some time in the 1980s and settled down into the safety and comfort of academia after traveling the Florida Keys and Pan Handle with her first husband.

She was a vegetarian and didn't wear leather in any form or fashion. Her second husband was too and they lived a quiet existence now going to work and coming home to their chalet-like retreat built of cedar to match the pines of the wooded 3 acres it sat on, off the beaten path gravel road where they aspired to be left alone, bird watch, feed the deer and have their dogs...keeping the ravaged and hungry world with all its toxins at bay.

though the two sisters seemed like they were two different ends of the spectrum as fas as style and career were concerned, they had similarities that would normally go unseen to the naked eye or at an initial meeting when sometimes people may mistake them for friends versus siblings.

With the age gap of the Beatles for Laura and Aerosmith for Tess, they were close and shared a kinship that only two people born of the same mother and raised together could. And while each had operated autonomously in their adult lives due to distance and proximity, they supported one another vicariously and were always only a phone call away. Unfortunately, now Laura would be on the receiving end of Tess's call from jail!

No Panties! No Bra! And No Socks for You!
Their afternoon Free Time passed quickly...women at the meal tables playing cards, talking, getting drinks, heating up things in the microwave, reading remnants of the Atlanta Journal Constitution, doing laps around the Pod.

The guard called "Pill Call!...if you don't get pills, go stand by your door."

"Ladies, clear liquid only. You know that by now!"

"Pill call! Pill call! Line up alphabetically."

Tess seemed a little jumpy at the command and a woman with short curly black hair and glasses who was sitting quietly reading at the same table looked up. "...it's for those who have to take pills." she stated the obvious. "Just go stand by your door and wait until they're through and then we can go back to our 'recess.'" she mocked and rolled her eyes with a slight smile.

As she got up, the woman revealed a tall, lanky frame. Tess thought the woman odd, not because of anything strange about her, but because she seemed so normal. So normal.

Kitty was a schoolteacher. Soft spoken and demure in her mannerisms, but not that feminine, which was also a dichotomy as far as Tess's impression of her was concerned.

She was in jail for a probation violation. "You know, a V.O.P." and Tess had to ask in her stupidly as to what that was. She was on probation for her second D.U.I. which she knew she had been in the wrong to do, even though it was a minimal amount she had had to drink at the time.

"The officer asked me if I had been drinking and I told him 'Yes, I had a couple of beers at lunch.' which had been a few hours before."

"He didn't even test me and I got the D.U.I. just because I admitted to having the beers. I wasn't drunk at all. I had eaten and everything. I was on probation for my first D.U.I., so that's all that mattered. I shouldn't have had anything to drink at all...period." she explained, seemingly happy to have someone to talk to.

"But I'm here now because I moved out of state to be with my boyfriend and came by the probation office to put my address change in and they arrested me and put me in here."

"That doesn't sound right." Tess interjected.

"I had spoken to my probation officer at the time when I was planning to move and he gave me the ok. Now he's not there anymore and they're saying they don't have proof of my going to D.U.I. school or the hours of Community Service I've done. I can't believe all this!"

Tess sympathized.

"I have all the paperwork. My Mom is getting it for me. I told them I had it. I've paid all my fines. I've done everything they wanted me to do! All I want to do it get out of this county and get out of Georgia!" She held her forehead and shook it back and forth. "It sounds like it will all work out because you have all your paperwork." Tess tried to reassure her.

"Yes, I know. It's just hard being in here and my boyfriend's in Missouri." she whined. "That's where I was going to be moving...to be with him. It's just really hard. I can't believe they've got this 'hold' on me and I have to sit here."

"You can't bond out?" Tess asked innocently.

"No, not with a V.O.P. Not with a 'hold.' I have to wait for a court date. So, I'm just reading a lot."

Tess talked to Kitty for a while until the afternoon Free Time was over at 2:45, then back to the room or cell...whatever you want to call it!

Staci asked who Tess had gotten in touch with and she gave her a report. Tess asked Sissy about her charges and got a vague reply of "Doin' somethin' I wasn't supposed to be doin'." followed by her signature giggle.

"I still have my job when I gets outta heres. They already told me I do." she said proudly.

"That's wonderful." Tess said sincerely. "Where do you work?"

"At da Taco Bell on Hickory Flat." Sissy informed. "My sister work there too and it's also a chicken place."

"What do you do there?"

"I's a cook."

"And you like it?"

"Oh, I like it fine. It pay better than the Bojangles. I was there before Taco Bell."

"Well, it sure sounds like they value you as an employee and want you back when you get out." Tess encouraged her.

"They do...they really do." Sissy confirmed with a smile forgetting to cover her mouth. "My boss got my check and had it put on my books for here too!"

"Books?" Tess didn't follow.

Staci chimed in, taking a break from picking at her hair, in the mirror plate, again. "Your books, you know, your account with the jail."

Tess shook her head. She didn't know.

"Oh yeah! You don't know nothin'! You never been to jail." Staci shouted stamping her foot.

"She aint never been to jail." she said to Sissy.

"Shoot girl, you really don't. Ok, listen..." Staci took her seat at the desk stool and leaned over, hands on her knees ready to explain...

"When you get booked...you know, arrested...if you have any money on you...in your pockets or purse or whatever...they either put it in your property or on your books. Some jails are different...may do one or the other. If you got money on your book you can go to the store and buy stuff...food, shampoo, socks. There's a sheet you order from every week."

"Store comes every Tuesday. You have to have your order in by Thursday. You need to get your family to send you money to put on there if you don't have any. You missed this week's store though." she explained.

Staci began rummaging through her plastic bin and pulled out a piece of paper and handed it to Tess. It offered everything from Ladies Speed Stick deodorant ($3.90), to one bar of soap ($1.50), dental floss ($2.60), denture tablets ($4.48), ibuprofen ($0.40), to clothing...t-shirt ($3.84), one pair of socks ($1.96), thermal top and bottoms ($7.98 each), one pair of panties ($2.98).

Toiletries, under garments, paper and pencil, cards, plastic cup and bowl, instant coffee, sweet and low, mayonnaise packets, tea, lemonade and punch packets, cookies, chips, ramen noodles, popcorn, tuna, pickles, rice and more.

"Wow!" Tess marveled. "All the comforts of home!" They all laughed.

"But, gosh, it's like Highway Robbery! The prices are outrageous." She marveled.

"Yea, girl. It's all about the money. Whether it's the commissary, fines, probation or what, they're gonna git ya!" Staci attested.

"I think you were in the wrong con, Staci." Tess laughed. "You should be running the jail store!"

They laughed. Sissy continued, "Cherokee County gets something like $150-$300 a day per inmate here. They be trying to pay for this new jail. It's only a few years old!"

"Really? Wow. Very enlightening. Our tax dollars at work." Tess added. "Maybe I can get some socks, underwear and toothpaste."

"You didn't get any underwear or bra?" Sissy asked, looking up from her Bible, having switched from Vampires to Apostles.

"Uh, no! Can you believe that?"

"They should have at least given you some panties! God! They so cheap around here." Sissy shook her head.

"You can get some temporary panties," Sissy told her. "From the guard. It's to hold a pad when you's got your time."
Tess nodded.

"They make a good eye mask too!" Staci remarked.

"The pad?"

"No, girl. The panties!" Staci laughed and held up a 3"x6" woven square and tossed them at Tess on her mat on the floor.

"So tell me a little more about your case." Staci inquired, peering intently through her small wire rimmed glasses. She pursed her lips as she held her head in one hand.

Tess told her about the conversation with her sister and that an attorney was to come see her.

"What's going to happen next is you are going to go before a judge...a municiple judge and get formally charged. Then, you'll be given a bond. It's your 72-hour hearing...they have 72 hours to charge you."

"Oh, I see." Tess murmured, thinking "You should get a bond. It doesn't sound like they have anything on you...so just wait it out for a few days and that's it...you'll be home."

Relieved, Tess said, "Oh, I really hope so. I've got to get home and get back to work."

"Yeah Baby, I know you do."

Do you want bread with that?
Dinner was served at 4:00 and the doors were automatically opened with a call from the guard of "Trays are on the floor!" coming like clockwork. The ladies on top came down and those from the bottom went obediently up and around as before. Tess felt like a zombie just going through the motions (again) and found her seat at the same table as before from lunch...this would be "her" seat from now on.

Staci and "her" table were right below Tess's, but no vacancies, so she didn't want to create any unrest. Sandy, the dike, sat at the head of Tess's table again and Pam, with her fountain of grey hair, bushy eyebrows and four teeth, asked politely if Tess wanted her pudding...or jello...or awfully dry cake concoction...depending on the offering. She promised she'd be the first to get it if she didn't want it.

A very pretty younger girl with contrasting blonde highlights in her fairly dark hair was a new arrival. Her skin was unseasonably bronze Tess noticed as she picked at her food and scowled, "Gross!" poking at the spiral noodle entre with some type of brown gravy on it.

"I'll take it if you're not going it eat it," Sandy hungrily announced.

"You can have it!" she frowned with a pout. "I don't even know why I even got out of bed for this."

"Can I have your puddin'?" Pam asked, her eyes brightening.

"Take whatever you want! This shit is gross!" the girl bitched, pushing her tray forward and removing herself from the table. She was scarecrow thin and the uniform barely hung off her.

"She better eat or she's just going to waste away," the larger woman to Sandy's right added. "It's not the best but it's all we get."

"She'll learn." Sandy said. "I don't get no Store." she rationed scooping the noodle mess onto her tray. "...and I gotta eat!" she smiled and laughed.
"I gotta eat!" she grinned grabbing the two pieces of bread too.

Tess just watched and tried to eat her noodles, but could only bear a few. The accompanying side of carrots, although mushy, were welcome, and she nibbled a piece of bread thankful it was wheat this time and not stale.

Another woman at the table had taken her bread and crumbled it up, mixing it and her carrots in with the noodles with a Rachel Ray flair for culinary artistry. She began shoveling the concoction in her mouth, elbow out, in a mechanical way.

She informed Tess of this interesting fact, "We usually get two pieces of bread at every meal. That's six pieces of bread a day. Even if you average that at four a day...if we get cornbread or a biscuit on one meal...that's still 24 pieces of bread a week! A whole loaf easy!"

"Whoa! That's a lot of bread!" Tess was surprised.

"So much for a low carb diet in here!" she mused, making a mental note not to eat the noodles or any bread if she could help it.

"Tess! Tess!" she heard her name whispered. Looking around in surprise there was Diana! Tess's eyes grew large and she gasped! Diana looked disheveled and her hair was a major fright!

"Ok ladies! If you're done with your tray, return to your room!" the guard announced. Obediently the inmates followed each other and did what they were told.

Tess and Diana walked together with trays in hand.

"Oh my God! You're in here too!" Diana exclaimed, excited, nervous and still confused by it all.

"Yes, and with no bond." Tess said discouraged. "But at the 72-hour hearing we're supposed to get one."

"All our things are at the house...my purse...my cell phone...everything I own..." Diana cried.

"I've never been in any trouble at all. My family's going to be mortified and totally devastated by all this."

"I know! Mine too!" Tess commiserated.

"I've got grandchildren." Diana moaned. This Grandmother was sure a sight in her orange jail scrubs!

"OK Ladies! Finish your trays and return to your rooms!" the guard ordered again, beginning to get impatient, the women lingering. A few inmates were still seated and eating, with others standing around their doors and talking.

"Keep the noise level down!" the guard yelled and the volume automatically came down a few notches.

"What room are you in?" Tess asked her.

"I'm in 10." Diana answered anxiously.

"I'm in 3." Tess confirmed. "We're just a few doors away from each other."

The two walked to their respective doors, desperately wanting to talk but not being given the chance because it was lockdown again!

"Lockdown Ladies! Lockdown!"

Tess was frustrated as she told Staci about seeing Diana. "Why do they always lock us down? It's like we're criminals or something!" she complained.

Staci looked at her over the top of her glasses down her nose, "Girl, we are criminals!" and they laughed.

"Ok, ok." Tess said, embarrassed.

Staci continued, "Some of the other jails are better than this. In Cobb (County) the food is A LOT better. You get free time all the time and no lockdown. They issue you more clothes, something to sleep in. The uniforms are better and you get a sweatshirt, different shirts and socks...stuff like that."

"They have an open Pod too! And, more phones too! Shoot, this place only got 4 phones for over 60 women. It's ridiculous!"

"Yeah, this place....this place is shit! But, the women in here ain't nothin' to worry about...all petty shit. At least it's clean because it ain't that old, you know..." she continued.

"And their store in Cobb isn't such a rip off. You can order more at a time and it's half the price of what they sell things for in here!"

"They got some racket going on here, for sore!" Sissy chimed in. "Makin' you buy flannels just so you can stay warm."

"It's all about the money, Baby. All about the money." Staci confirmed.

"I'm starting to see that." Tess nodded in agreement.

"Yeah, I think they just keeps people in here for as long as they can, for whatever they can, just to get their per diem per inmate, you know what I mean?" Sissy added.

"When do we get out again?" Tess asked.

"She let us out for free time again at 6:00 o'clock. We'll have a new guard then. It think it be Miss Chastain." And with that Staci announced she needed a nap..."her beauty rest, you know, Baby." and tied a sock around her head like a head band and settled back into her bunk with Sissy engrossed in her Bible up top, busily scratching it with a pencil. Tess asked her what she was doing and she said,

"Marking each verse with a colored pencil so I knows what I read."

Tess nodded and smiled at her, laid down on her mat on the floor until six.

Low Life Saga

The doors buzzed and clicked their three time rhythm and the dimmed lights of the rooms brightened for the evening, offering their limited "freedom."

Staci didn't budge, but Sissy happily swung her long legs down from the bunk to the desk top and with a quick 1-2-3 was down on the floor and on to the toilet. Tess tried not to notice as she relieved herself and the stood up to stretch.

Tess hadn't been able to sleep, but did get a little rest. She thought about Evan and wondered how he was. She imagined him somewhere similar to this, somewhere nearby in this maze of a building.

"I gots to call my sister." Sissy said. "Miss Chastain always do a phone list at night so everybody gets a turn."

"Git up girl!" she ordered Staci, furrowing her eyebrows. "You don't want to get in trouble, dos ya?"

Staci stirred, rubbing her eyes as she pulled the blanket from above her head.

The women inmates all stood outside their doors as a pretty blonde with her hair pulled back tightly stood in the open area before them. At ease, with her hands clasped behind her back. Tess noticed her heavy eye make-up and lipstick and felt like she was mocking their plainness.

As all the women began to emerge and stand quietly, the Deputy began to walk slowly back and forth like an attorney in motion ready to cross examine.

"Ok, is everybody out?" she asked with a shrill and very country sounding twang that made Tess raise an eyebrow.

"Git your asses outta them beds!" she chirped, continuing to pace.

"Everybody come on and have a seat down here!" she said, motioning with her arms.

"Come on! Come on...you girls don't need to be slow like some herd of cows or something! We ain't got all night!" she complained.

"Let's get this over with so you can have your free time!"

Everyone made their way to the tables and Tess scanned the group finding Diana again amongst the sea of orange. They greeted each other with a hug and sat down together at one of the tables.

The murmuring of the women turned into a rumble and Officer Chastain shouted, "Quiet!" while several of them "shushed" the others. When the talking silenced, Miss Chastain began her speech.

"Ok everybody. Let's get this show on the road here." As she got closer in her pacing, Tess could see the shimmer of her dramatic eye make-up of silver and smokey grey and the big black lashes waving as she blinked.

She could have been an Avon or Mary Kay representative about to address her captive audience of plain Janes who probably would have done just about anything for some lip gloss, concealer, moisturizer and mascara at this point.

"I'm Officer Chastain, or Miss Chastain. I'm pretty easy going compared to some of the guards in here with you gals. You give me respect, I'll do the same for you and we'll get along just fine."

"I've got at thing about the noise level in here. I'll give you a warning, but after that you're going to lose 5 minutes each time to lockdown at 9:30...so you better keep it quiet...as quiet as 60 women can be with all your yaking!"

"Oh wow! She was actually making a joke!" Tess laughed to herself, entertained by this Miss Chastain.

"I don't need to hear you hootin' and hollerin' squallerin' like children if you know what I mean? I also don't need to see your panties hanging all over your rooms and shit hanging all over the place. I know you all do your laundry in here...you get your garbage cans and wash your underthings...but I don't want to walk past these rooms and see everybody's underwear! If you've got them hangin', you need to get them down! Understand!"

A solemn "Yes Ma'am!" answered followed by a few giggles and talking. "Ssssh! Sssssh!" randomly fluttered through the group.

Tess looked at Diana, her hair still wild and disheveled as it was when she had seen her walk by in the booking area...but now she had it pushed off her face as best she could and kept pushing it back and twisting the back into a bun that wouldn't stay, nervous and seeming a bit irritated.

"I need a hair tie." she whispered apologetically.

Officer Chastain continued..."As far as panties go, they belong on your ass and not your head!" she yelled, directing at the black women. The group laughed.

She was on a roll now and gave off a hint of a smile. "I ain't got no pads or temporary underwear tonight, so don't ask."

"Visitation is tonight and there will be a list posted on my desk. You can come up and look at it. Don't keep coming up to me asking 'Do I have visitation? Do I have visitation?'" she mimicked in a whiney voice and made a face. The women laughed like canned laughter on a sitcom and were quickly silent again.

Tess watched her stride and noticed how tight her pants fit and that she had a decent figure. She thought Miss Chastain was a pistol and seemed "human" versus some of the drones she'd come across so far.

She imagined Miss Chastain was probably quite something in the police officer clique around here, with many male officers vying for her attention. But as attractive as she appeared, her voice was what struck her. Once she opened her mouth, it was over. She was so country it wasn't even funny!

"Now we're going to have a phone list tonight. You girls...I'm warning you all right here and now...if there's any squallering over them damn phones or any problem at all, I'm gonna take them away from everybody and that's a promise!" she warned them pointing her finger at the group and squinting her eyes.

"These phones are here for you to call your attorneys and that's it! It's a privilege you're given to use them to call your families. As sure as I'm standin' here tonight, I'll yank those phones so quick if I hear the first little bit of bitchin' and you know I will do it!"

A wave of a murmur spread through the room and Tess looked at Diana and raised her eyebrows in question.

"Have you called anybody?" Diana asked in a whisper.

"Yes, earlier." Tess answered.

"I've got to call my family." Diana whimpered, sounding desperate.

Chastain continued..."And you WILL BE getting the movie cart for the weekend!" she proclaimed with a big smile and the women applauded and cheered, whooping and hollering.

"Yes. Yes." she said proudly, nodding her head. "You all did real good last week and got the movie cart! Keep up the good work, Ladies! You have the cleanest Pod here!" smiling still.

"Ok, I'm done now. You can go about your business. The phone list starts with room 17 and 18 and goes from there!"
A few women made their way over to the phone bank and quickly sat down and started dialing, while a group gathered around the tv monitor on a media cart at the utility room across from the main door and guard's desk which housed their entertainment for the next 48 hours in the form of a DVD player!

Diana, still in shock from the preceding events, shared her experience with Tess in alarmed excitement. They shared the similarities of their experiences, the raids, the surprise and Diana rebuffed what Tess had feared...it was not their rental house that was the grow house.

Diana and Brian had changed course midway to move into another house Evan had taken charge of.

It had been leased by a friend of Evan's, JR, a big, burly fellow who was a former auto mechanic, tow truck driver and carpet layer before that. JR now had a bad back and unable to do the manual labor as before.

He was a jolly sort, boisterous and always with a story to tell, a former marine with tattoos on his forearms to prove it and he maintained a shaved head since his military days, but now donned small loop earrings that made him look like a cross between Popeye and a genie.

Evan had helped JR out of a jam (as usual) when he was in the process of a divorce, needed work (as usual) and a homeowner of a very nice two story traditional near the lake needed someone to finish the renovations and could occupy the residence. The house had been sitting empty for over a year thanks to a down market for the older resales, particularly those that were outdated and over-priced, of which this one was both!

JR had been there for the last year as he tried to separate himself from a trailer park, white trash wife, her pregnant teen daughter and derelict son who had been weighing him down like an anchor around his neck.

He'd been on a downward spiral ever since the two had gotten together. Tess thought JR was "ok" but couldn't stomach his chain smoking wife who, on the limited occasion, when she ran into was often out in public still in her house shoes!

Evan tried to help the step-daughter after she had her baby when the girl would call begging for work...anything...she'd clean the house, rake leaves...whatever...anything. But he'd have to go pick her up and bring her home because she still wasn't old enough to drive.

Her father died several years prior and Evan had been a friend of his. He took on the young girl as a family friend and tried to offer her guidance and support as he could. But it was a losing battle to try to change what she learned from her mother...to be a trailer wife, live off welfare and food stamps...or better still, a stipend or pension received after the father's death of some $900 per month.

And, the girl had no intention of getting her G.E.D. and now a few years older, worked at being a fully developed young whore looking to score meth and party with the best of them. She ended up working at Waffle House which was a good fit for her...Waffle House Wench! She made great tips!

Evan and Tess had talked about this sad family before, especially when she'd remind him that she really didn't want them to come out to the farm and Evan in his overly gregarious way would inevitably invite them over to swim in their "cement pond."

She lectured him again and again, pleaded... how she wanted him to have a better caliber of friends or acquaintances. He was better than that. SHE was better than that. He would vehemently argue that he was only trying to offer some type of guidance and good example to his dead friend's little girl.

Evan was always an advocate for the under-privileged and downtrodden. Always looking to see the good in people. Tess thought he was naive, and his good nature and kindness taken advantage of.

She remembered her mother's assessment of him as Lil' Abner which made her laugh. He didn't wear the overalls though! But Evan wasn't a simpleton. He just had a very sweet nature, was the offspring of basic, salt of the earth, country folk, but had evolved from there. He knew hardship and being poor. So, if he was able, he was adamant that if he wanted to help someone, he would and there was no point in arguing. Tess had tried.

"As long as you don't have them over." Tess conceded. She loved Evan (and love is blind) but she was starting to see his biggest attribute of being a caring and compassionate person as one of his biggest flaws, taking it too far with no boundaries for his family, for her.

In recent months Evan started to realize that the mother and daughter charity case were both into meth and he washed his hands of them rather quickly, as had JR. Now JR was trying to rebuild his life again and be something other than trash. Even with all his apparent shortcomings, if he had anything left at all, he had his pride.

JR was proud of the house he was now in. Proud of his skills and the work he had been able to do there. A mansion in comparison to the dingy metal trailer he had lived in, leased month to month or even week to week.

Evan was proud too. Proud to be able to help a friend and proud to have helped elevate JR out of the bowels of trailer parks and meth, food stamps and W.I.C. programs, DFACS, 14 year old mothers who innocently thought they knew it all, and a wife whose only power was between her legs and knew JR was a sucker for it.

JR held strong and they were divorcing. He wanted more in his life. He enjoyed the big house and was very gung-ho...at first. But the owner began complaining to Evan, acting as property manager of sorts (and he recommended the big oaf), about a poorly taken care of yard, old newspaper rolls still in the soggy plastic left in the drive, smoking in the house, trash in the garage, oil spills and a just plain "I don't care" type of attitude in general. JR had proven that the house was too much for him, just as a better woman would be, and had been asked to move out.

This is how Diana and Brian had ended up at that house. JR had moved out the day before and they were moving their things in. Little did they know they were moving in right on top of "300 marijuana plants" growing in the basement.

"Oh My God!" Tess said, obviously oblivious. Diana shook her head and bowed it with regret. "We were there moving our stuff in, cleaning, trying to get settled." Brian's mom was there helping too. JR and his wife were moving their things out as we were moving in."

"His wife was there?" Tess was surprised.

"We were only there for one night," Diana cried, "and the agents busted in and said, 'Can't you smell the marijuana?' and I said, 'No, I smell cleaning fluid.' I never smelled anything."

"Then they had us take a urine test and then tried to ask me and Brian all sorts of questions and when I told them I wouldn't talk to them without an attorney, they brought me here."

"I just can't believe this. I've never even had a traffic ticket and I'm a grandmother!"

"Me either," Tess agreed and just shook her head thinking, how could she not have known. How could they both not have known what was really going on with Evan and Brian and JR and those low lifes?

Does "dumb" hold up in Court?

Two innocent and dumb women who should have known better, but for love of two very charismatic guys, both very different, but each with their own merits of attraction. Now here they were.

Tess's mind raced. Thinking back, it made sense. Evan being gone all the time. The people he surrounded himself with. She was better than this. Look where it got her. Unbelievable!

She had to grapple with the reality that Evan used her. Used her resources. Her hard work. Her elderly mother. All to benefit low lifes. To grow pot! She was blown away!

She was mad at herself. How could she have not known?

How could she have given Evan chance after chance?

How could she have put her 20 years of hard work, 401k, savings, credit on the line, thinking about the $15k lines of credit at Home Depot and Lowe's that were maxed out, the 401k funds almost all gone, a $3200 a month note on the farm from an interest only 100% jumbo (predatory) Countrywide loan.

How could she get out of this! And the animals!

"We'll be out of here soon." Tess tried to comfort her as they both sat aimlessly looking around the pod, practically a ghost town now with most of the residents crammed into the small utility room watching their movie reward.

"What room are you in and how's your roommate?" Tess asked.

"Oh, I'm in 9 with a nice woman named Jan. She's here waiting to go to prison."

"Prison?" Tess asked concerned.

"She's very sweet. She was sleeping today and whoa, boy can she snore!"

"What's she in for?" Tess was curious.

"Oh, um, she poisoned her husband who had abused her for years. Finally couldn't take it anymore." Diana said matter of factly.

Tess's eyebrows raised. She'd have to meet Jan.

"That gives me some ideas!"

"Me too!"

The two laughed. "Let's go see what movie they're showing."

They walked across the Pod to the darkened utility room filled with the others sitting in the two rows of plastic chairs. The blaring audio accosted them as they opened the door to enter, all eyes glued to the glowing TV monitor, no one even glancing up at them.

Tess and Diana quietly stood inside by the door. The room was warm and stuffy from all the bodies and breathing, with the pungent odor of popcorn mixed with B.O. hanging in the thick air. A violent scene played out on the screen with "oohs" and "aahs" coming from the group.

"Oh my Lord!" someone yelled as the abuse scene played out with JLo taking punches and being thrown around a room by her actor-husband in the film, "Enough." Tess watched the expressions of the audience in the reflective light as some winced and shrunk down in their seats, while others stared blankly immune to the violence, and some covered their eyes at the all too familiar scene.

They jeered and cursed the accuser and talked back to him. A black girl who looked like a boy stood up in defense and shouted, "Hey Motherfucker! You can't do my JLo like dat! Come on! I'll kick your ass you bastard!"

"Shut the fuck up, Kilo. Sit down." another yelled.

"Shssh! Shssh!" the women hissed and the film rolled on.

"Do you want to watch this?" Diana whispered.

"No, I've seen it." Tess answered and the two ducked out quietly.

"I'm not really into seeing something like that. Especially here." Diana admitted.

"Me either." Tess agreed, thinking it ironic and inappropriate for the movie choice. She wondered if the same movie was also offered/shown to the men?

"Was Jan in there?" she asked.

"No, she's in the room." Which was probably a good thing.

They made their way over to the phone bank and inquired as to where they were in relation to the list and sat with a small group who decided to use their free time to call vs. watch "Enough."

Kitty was there waiting and reading, in her own world. As they sat down, she looked up and greeted them with a big smile and a big "Hello!" happy to have some company.

Tess introduced Diana to Kitty and they began talking, asking the obligatory question, "What'd they get you for?" or "What are you doing in here?"

Kitty told Diana about her D.U.I. and probation violation for moving out of state and also told the girls about her long-distance relationships with Steve...a nice fellow in Missouri who she met online in a poker chat room/web site.

Kitty had had other online romances, but Steve was her prize and prince and the separation and not even being able to I.M. each other was killing her. She was currently going through withdrawals. Steve withdrawals.

"I can handle not having cigarettes, but not being to talk to Steve is unbearable." she cried. "I'm waiting to get on a damn phone. This is ridiculous." Her upstart rant cut short by an announcement by Miss Chastain.

"The next set of visitors for Mathews, Kirk, Brown and Stevenson. You have visitation at 8:30."
Diana looked frantically at Tess. "Someone from my family has come to see me. Probably my daughter. Oh my God!" she said nervously.

"Damn!" Kitty exclaimed. The two of them looked at her concerned and asked what she was upset about.

"It's my mother. She's here for visitation and I just really don't want to hear it."

"Is she not supportive?" Tess asked.

"Well, she's supportive, but she's just so damn judgmental. I'm friggin' forty years old and I really don't need her trying to tell me what to do!"

"That's what mother's do, don't they?" Tess challenged her, thinking she should be glad someone cared enough about her to even come visit.

"Sure, but I'm just tired of it. She doesn't want me to move. She doesn't approve of Steve. You know, I've been married before, out on my own since I was in my twenties..."

"I'm sure she just cares about you, that's all." Diana added. "Do you have any children?"

"No, but I've got my cats. Six of them. They are my babies." Kitty explained and Tess was amused by the connection of her name and demeanor and the fact that here was this typical spinster-type school teacher, cat lady who, from what it sounded like had taken a dormant sex life to new heights thanks to the internet and a poker fetish.

She asked Kitty if her mom knew about her internet escapades.

"There's a lot she doesn't know about me." she said defiantly in her soft voice and tepid demeaner peering out innocently behind her glasses.

"Um, like what? Did you get a tattoo?" Tess quipped, laughing.

"No, I don't have any tattoos," she answered and Tess was a little disappointed but perked right back up when Kitty said, "But, I had my nipples pierced!"

"What!" Tess exclaimed, super surprised. "No way, Kitty!"

"Yes, way!" she assured her. "It's something I've always to do."

"Really?" Tess questioned, amazed and somewhat in shock. "Did it hurt? And, um, why?" she asked, very curious.

Kitty beamed and smiled a devious little grin, "I always wanted to do it...I'm not sure why...but I just went into this tattoo piercing place that I'd always drive by and told the guy what I wanted."

"I sat there in the chair, took off my top and bra and he just stuck the needle right through my nipple, then did the other one. There wasn't really much to it." she explained.

"He wasn't so sure about me when I first came in and warned me about flinching and the pain, but it didn't even hurt. It just burned a little. I didn't flinch one bit. Not at all!"

Tess and Diana were mesmerized.

"I guess that's something your mother doesn't know about!" Diana commented.

"Oh no! I mean, I don't go around showing them to anybody." Kitty attested.

"I'll bet Steve likes them!" Tess jabbed.

"Oh yes, he really does. I'm thinking about getting something else pierced." Kitty confessed, looking down. They all laughed and said, "Oh!"

"I'm completely clean." Tess said proudly. "No tattoos, piercings...other than my ears. I'm just not into it. Maybe if I was younger? I just don't get it. I couldn't have something on my body...for the rest of my life. Some graphic or image. I'd get tired of it."

"Oh no! I'm not getting anything tattooed or pierced. No way!" Diana stated adamantly.

"Leviticus 19:28, You shall not make any cuts in your flesh, nor Tattoo any marks on your body." she quoted.

"Hey Kitty," Tess exclaimed, "When your mom is getting on your case, tell her that there's a lot she doesn't know about you and announce that you got your nipples pierced and just pull up your top and flash her!"

"Oh My God! She'd have a heart attack." Kitty mused, her eyes glazing over as the wheels of her brain worked in devious delight imagining the scene.

"I just might do that!" she said with a keen smile, taking a sip of her red kool-aid and looking off into space still smiling.

The Net is Cast

"8:30 visitation. Let's go ladies!" Chastain yelled. "Get a move on. We ain't got all night."

Tess reassured Diana that it would be "okay" and watched her and Kitty make their way up the stairs to the visiting area above where they could talk to whoever cared enough to come via the double glass observation windows and play phone receivers.

Now alone at the table, Tess turned her attention to the phone where Staci was happily chatting and laughing amongst the other three women huddled into the small corners of their respective booths. A young girl was crying, her face red and eyes forlorn. Tess recognized her from the table where they had shared a meal and felt sorry for her.

"Sanderson...Room 3...phone!" a girl called out at the next opening and Tess quickly jumped over to the phone. She would call the farm tonight and check on things and see if they had heard from Evan.

Everything was being taken care of, she found out. The animals were all fine. The horses and dogs all doing well. Everyone was concerned for her. Evan had called and said he loved her, would get her out of this mess and not to worry. Some consolation she thought sarcastically, but it was good to hear and she had no choice but to take him at his word...whatever that was worth!

There had been searches, Frank told. Apparently everyone Evan knew had been questioned. Their homes searched in the same manner using the "home invasion", surprise technique with the assumption that these hard-working mostly blue collar folks were drug users, dealers or manufacturing cohorts.

Everyone Evan had had contact with, any dealings with over the last six months. The assumption was guilt first and they searched diligently to find anything at all to connect them with drugs or marijuana. They even urine tested everyone to be sure and still came up empty handed.

The drug task force called the C-men were on the hunt and it appeared that this lengthy investigation had yielded little and definitely not what they had thought. If they thought Evan was some big time drug dealer, Tess knew they were barking up the wrong tree. If anything, he was very SMALL TIME. "I talked to Nardelli at your office and am fielding your real estate calls over to him." DeeDee informed her, sounding very official and business-like, even with her strong southern drawl. "He knows what's going on and he's cool."

"He's handling Tonia, the client you were working with and is going to take her over to the property you recommended. Also a fellow, Tom Ross, is interested in a $600k property you emailed him. I told him you had a family emergency and would be back in a week or two. I tried to send him to Bob, but he said he only wanted to work with you...would wait...wasn't in a rush."

Tess's mind swirled around like it was in a blender with all the real estate properties, leads, prospects and clients she had been working on. Thank God Deb had her cell phone! Her business lifeline. And thank God she had trained her in the business some and she was so good at handling things. She thanked God for Deb and Frank. The "hand-up" they had been given was well worth it and paying off in a way she could never have imagined.

Tess had created her own groove as far as the real estate was concerned, incorporating her marketing strategies learned from her mentor, a Harvard MBA and Atlanta advertising CEO and marketing guru who she had worked with as an Executive Assistant when she first started in the world of business some 20 years past.

Armed with the ability to write, type and computers skills, he dictated and paced and barked out commands in his flattering Australian accent while she put together proposals, presentations and articles for some of the top companies and brands in the region. With every project they worked on, Tess learned. She learned through osmosis from her charismatic boss and liked to say she got HER MBA this way.

She worked tirelessly from deadline to deadline, meeting to meeting, hoping for more recognition, but was only seen as an Admin. She knew it would be worth it in the long run, the projects were interesting and she was always learning and growing. One day she would make him proud and make him notice that she was smart and had been a good apprentice, even if he didn't see it all the time.

The real estate web site she made herself, as a showcase of all the horse farms for sale in the area. Tess made it easy and informative and it was what her niche was looking for. It didn't splash her face all over the place, nor did it tout some ABC Realty and who is better than XYZ because of this, that or the other. Before "reciprocity" came into play where agents could promote other agent's listings, she ran into some opposition, particularly in little Cherokee County, but that didn't phase her. She was not here to make friends. She was here to get clients and make money.

A call or two or three from a disgruntled agent, angry and challenging her as to why "their" listing was on "her" web site. Again, this was then...before Zillow...10+ years before. She was definitely ahead of the real estate tech-curve.

Her horse farm web site was just what her type of buyers wanted...a site where they could find a home where they could have their animals. Her labor of love was working and it gave her the option of taking over this lucrative niche, as the other local agents were still scrambling with the changes in the industry, reciprocity and the MLS and Realtor.com had yet to get up to speed.

Hundreds of hits a week with no advertising or monies paid for what we now call SEO. Only $50 per month for her web hosting and great qualified leads, more than she could handle. Her mentor Alf, indeed, had taught her well.

"Ok, listen Sug," Dee twanged, "We've got it all covered. I'm working the real estate end of things for you. Frank's got the horses taken care of. Boy it's sure a good thing you showed him what to do with them when you did...I tell you what!"

"But, you don't worry your pretty little head about nothin', you hear...you just take care of yourself in there and Evan's gonna get you out of this whole darned thang! He's real upset. All's he's concerned about is getting you out so you don't lose everything!"

"No! No! I don't want to lose anything!...all I've worked so hard for." Tess cried.

"You won't! You won't!" Dee reassured her. "We'll beat this crap. It's all gonna be alright. Don't you worry now." and the phone call ended with three beeps...their time was up.

Tess rubbed her head, still reeling. She thought about her Broker Bob and what he must think of all this. God, all the business she had and not being able to do anything. All the money she was losing being stuck in jail!

"Man, this sucks!" she said out loud as she got up from the phone, coming back to reality of where she was and the stark reality of how she got there.

"You got that right!" Staci agreed, putting her arm around Tess's shoulders and the two walked back to Room 3.

Letters: Tess, Mom and Evan

January 10th,

Dear Mom,
This is all so surreal. It is a test in strength and tolerance. I try to imagine what you are going through as I go through various stages of this surprising incarceration I now find myself in. It was certainly tumultuous at first. Very scary and shocking. Unbelievable. A nightmare you can't wake from. But, I've made it through to this point and am "okay."

I've had to put it in God's (and my attorney's) hands to make this right and trust things will all work out.

I was placed in the Medical section the first day or two where nurses were uncaring and was totally isolated by design. I tried to stay calm, but so many things were racing through my mind and emotions were so strong, it was very difficult there. The worst part of this stay.

When brought into the Pod, J-Pod, at some time around 3:00 am I am placed in a very quiet area and rooms of sleeping women. I get room 3 with two black girls, Marian aka Sissy and Staci in the bunks. I am on the floor.

They turn out to be super sweet and one a legal ace with a 20 year history in the system from fraudulent activities like checks, credit cards or identity theft. I was able to learn a lot from her about our legal system, procedures, etc. and think I've been able to inspire her to possibly invest in real estate.

She's supposed to get out soon and vows it will be her last time in jail (or prison). I sure hope so. She has a lot of potential. She's smart, personable. I really hope she makes it!

Lots of crazy stories in here... mine being one of them! Haha I didn't realize what a police state we are living in in this "Land of the free," with so many rights being so blatantly violated and disregarded. I am not the only one. This is a strange comfort, yet a concern.

I won't go into the tirade of injustices and fabricated charges many have described. You can imagine. It's a pretty bad situation. Of course, most of the women are here for methamphetamine. That is also a really big problem. Most are so stupid too! And you know me... full of advice and telling many of my new found friends what they need to do or should do.

This place could really help these poor souls if they had counseling, some sort of vocational amenities... something! It's like nobody is even trying to fix the problem at all.
I guess it's such a cash cow for the county, why fix it? But I do believe that many could clean up their acts and really want to, but just can't do it alone.

On the other side of the coin, for many it is also a game, a way of life, exciting, some type of sub-culture... in and out of jail... hanging on the "outside"... blah, blah, blah. What a waste! Maybe they will all grow up eventually. Maybe I will too! haha

Now, after being here over a week, it's a routine. I'm starting to sleep a little better now that I've settled down some and have a bunk. My new roomie is a younger girl who is sweet, and we are now on a self-imposed (me) work out schedule. She's trying to lose some baby weight still hanging on from a year ago.

The food is not so great, but I'm thankful to get what I get! But I've sworn off the Kool-aid (real not figurative), any type of sweets and the bread! Oh the bread! Most of what we get is sugar and carbs...yuk!

I hope Evan is ok with his food. I worry about him. No sushi here! Haha

I should have said I was a vegetarian when I checked into this place! So, I'm going to try to stick with whatever veggies I can get, proteins and drink a lot of water. I'm sure I've lost some weight by now from the stress, so I might as well keep going with it until my hearing on the 19th and keep with the exercising. Maybe some good will come of all this, like getting skinny. Ha! What a way to lose weight! The J-Pod Diet!

Today is a positive day. There are surely extreme highs and lows in here. Of course I worry a lot about the state of my life once this is resolved and my name is cleared.

I worry and think about Evan a lot too and have tried not to be too angry with him and prayed for his well-being, safety and future. I have put the matter into God's hands and must trust and have faith regarding everything here.

We had such a wonderful life plan that seems like it really didn't get a chance to flower. I wonder about having a family and one day getting married...but first things first! Get out of jail first! Haha

It is still not something I am giving up on. I will have a happy life and one I have dreamed of. I am determined. I will not give up on that!

While I have felt confused, upset, defeated, and powerless in moments, I know those are fleeting emotions and justice will prevail with perseverance and positive thinking. I am NOT a criminal. I have done nothing wrong.

I am truly blessed with such a wonderful family and appreciate all that has been done on my behalf since this began. Thank you! Thank you! Thank you! From the bottom of my heart! Without you, my hope would have been completely lost. Also, the help at home as been a God Send. Thank you Frank and DeeDee!

I will have a lot to do once I get out of here! I hope I can salvage most of what was. I can't wait to see the dogs and the horses, my loves, be enveloped in the comforts of my wonderfully comfortable bed, eat some real food and best of all, be free! You can't put a price on that!

I am resting up now and gaining strength so I can fight the good fight for what I call my life and for those who have helped me, believed in me, and for the ones I love.

I will get through this, but not alone.

I am ok and working on a strong mind and body. (But my Chrons has flared up again. Hopefully cutting off the bread will help.) Biding my time for now.

With all my love,
Tess

PS - "I'm braless, pantiless with no tooth paste and no shampoo, whoa, whoa, in the Cherokee County Jail, what's a girl to do?" sounds like the next big country song! Haha

Dear Tess,

It is difficult to understand how this trouble could come on. Here you are working so hard to get your farm in order and finishing your Broker school and all, then this mess. I can only hope and pray that it will all be put straight and ok soon.

We will try best we can to help out - do anything we can. It's all so new to us that I just don't know what I'm doing and hope I do what's right.

I never wanted to be a millionaire until now...could really use it, right? Oh well, we'll do what we can.

Meanwhile, you keep calm as you can and say some extra prayers...it has to be ok...and soon...all will be right...soon. A $20 money order is enclosed.

Love you, Mom

Dear Love,

I would not trade my worst day with you for my best day with anyone else and that includes these times now. How can this be so hard for anyone to understand? I realize now that before you I would have never understood feelings like that myself. Do you remember when we first got together…how I would always let out a big breath of relief every time we were alone? It was and still is because there is no where I had rather be than alone with you. It is freedom. Freedom not only from the chains that bind me in every day life, but freedom for my heart to soar in any direction toward an endless horizon, farther than can be seen or even imagined.

All of our time together has been a gift. I did not pick you out. I asked for you, just like you asked for me.

As I just wrote those words down I realized how much more powerful the Universe is than any group of human beings. I hope we will both remember this during these troubled times as well as in the good times that will follow. Don't give up your dreams and ask for what you need. If you have to make decisions for us without me, know that I trust and support you.

Love always,
Evan

January 18th,

Dear Mom,
I received your letter today! Thanks for sending it! And for the encouraging words! I am so fortunate to have you and Sis in my corner, as well as the support from our family, although I wish we could have kept this embarrassment from them somehow. Oh well, it is what it is and we'll just have to get through it the best we know how. Right! ☺'

Jail Life has now become a routine and I'm doing my best to not freak out! I just hope and pray to be able to get out of here soon. I'll know more of my fate tomorrow/Friday at my bond hearing. Hope my laywer is as good as everyone says.

The Church Ladies came tonight. There are two sets of them…Baptists and Soul/Gospel. The Baptists are all fire and brimstone…they mean well, but are pretty scary. The black ladies are so awesome and I enjoy them and their energy. They get everybody going. They bring a boom box and cd's, and sing! They're really great! It's their calling to help the women in here! I think they really do make an impact.

It's been good to reconnect with God through their energy. Much different then my own solitary prayers.

I also got ahold of a book by the fellow on PBS, Wayne Dyer, about the power of intention...his view of praying/manifesting and getting closer to "the source." It's all good stuff. Maybe that's part of my purpose here...for me to appreciate, be humbled and get ready for my future as a more enlightened human being. I've pretty much turned it all over to God and am at peace. That's really all you can do.

We are so not in control of anything, really. Here is a cute saying from the book... "Good morning! This is God. I will be handling all of your problems today. I will not need your help, so have a miraculous day!"

I like that!

The gal in here who is the girlfriend of Evans friend who is also in trouble, she and I are becoming good friends. She, like me, was completely blindsided by this whole thing, is a grandmother, never been in any kind of trouble before. Her name is Diana and she's a little school-marm type. Very sweet. We joked around saying she's the head of this whole thing, Grandma Mathews and her gang. Haha

Not really that funny under the circumstances, but there she was standing with these really big burly biker type guys in court, and she's this 5 ft tall, little innocent lady, with her hair in a bun, glasses, etc. Any body with any sense at all could see there was something very wrong with that picture!

Diana is hanging in there too and her family is rallying around her. I'm sure we will be friends for life after going through this ordeal together.

It has been very difficult for both of us as our hopes and dreams with the men in our lives have come to a screeching halt. It all hangs in the balance and you question motives and if you can get any semblance of normalcy back? I trust it will be resolved, but right now it is a slow resolve. So slow.

I am very sad at the prospect of losing my sweet Evan and the life I hoped we could have together and any children we may be could have had. I would have loved to have a family with him, but I am afraid that now the time is lost. Even at my age now, I feel I am going into early menopause. Probably accelerated due to this stress.

So much wasted time. I so wish we could have some of it back! I wish Evan would have focused more on me and our relationship. I wish we could have had more joy and fun together. He was so absent for so long. It's a sad situation, especially when you love someone, know what a good person they are and just realize they were on a misguided path.

I thought I could help him to see his potential and be the man I knew he could be and he really wanted to be. But, if it's true what they are saying about him, he has let us all down. I can't believe he would risk so much...so, so much. Really everything that matters in this world, for something so stupid. I guess one of his friends egged him on? I just don't know.

He has so much potential, was going to help me with my real estate company and was so excited about that! Gosh, the real estate could make more money than what the authorities are saying of the pot stuff! It's ridiculous! I can't believe he put me/us in such a terrible position...such jeopardy. I don't want to believe it!

Hopefully, all is not what it appears. But, as they say, love is blind. I'm trying not to be blind any more.

Also, as they say, the truth will prevail. That is what I am praying for. Thank you so much for hanging in there. I am so sorry you and the family are having to deal with this mess! Thanks for standing by me and for supporting me in my innocence.

With all my love,
Tess

Dear Love,

How are you doing? I miss you terribly. I am sorry that you have had to go through all of this but I know it has made you stronger and appreciation of things just like it has done for me.

So what do we do now? That's not really that hard of a question. Let me first tell you again where I stand. All of the material things do not matter to me. Don't get me wrong, I have enjoyed them and like nice things but I won't lose any sleep over letting any of it go. I grew up poor and have started my life with nothing but a dream and ambition more than once.

I had rather live in a trailer with you than a mansion with anybody else. Even if we let go of everything we have and moved into a camper, do you think we would stay there long? You know we wouldn't. You or me by ourself would rise up an out of any poor circumstances fast and strong. Think how much faster things happen with the two of us together as a team.

I have supported you on everything you have wanted to do since I met you. The only thing I am not behind you on are decisions made in weakness or fear…reactions rather than actions. (I am not saying you are doing that, this is just my thought in general.)

You have a few tough decisions to make now with the horses and the future of the farm. The horses are totally your decision. To me, they are not just animals, they are my friends.

Any way, back to the point. We have to be realistic on what we have to work with. The sale of the tractor will buy you some time to decide which direction you want to go with your career and the farm. Don't forget to include who you are and what you are able to do in your list of resources. Also include me. At this time, I am not sure when I will be out and for how long, so I can only promise what I can do in here and what resources I currently have available out there.

Remember also there are some things I do no matter where I am. These are the same things that you can do also. Believe it.

What are the things that are really important to you? This is what you have to ask yourself and then answer yourself truthfully and honestly. Then and only then will your direction become clear. Only you know those answers…you and God.

I have asked myself that same question more than once in here and have each time come to the same conclusions…the things I asked for before all if this happened. Believe me, I have a clear head about things now. I will not put myself in the same positions that ultimately caused me to end up here. Not only were my time and resources being drained, but my orendi and my physical health were being drained as well.

As far as the farm is concerned, this I my opinion…if we can afford to keep it, pay back the money we had to borrow and have some left over each month to build up our savings, I am all for it.

I absolutely love the place and am willing to work hard for it and for you. But, I am not willing to be a slave to that much debt and not have time or money for you or anything else. I had rather live at the rental house or some place less expensive and enjoy live together and be able to spend time with you, go out to eat, etc. and be able to spend time and money with my son, our families including your mother and sister.

I believe we can do it all but I want to build a firm financial foundation before we jump too far ahead of ourselves again. We've got a month or so to decide. It is appealing to think of the sale of the tractor would pay for a year's worth of mortgages on the rental house. The utilities would be less as well. Think about what you want to do.

On another note, I am sending you a necklace a Mexican man in here made. Don't feel that you have to wear it or anything, I just thought it was cool and could e a reminder that I am always thinking of you. Hand in there and go give it your all!

Love always,
Evan

January 23rd,

Dear Mom and Sis,

I just received my "order" from the jail store and am very happy to have my own paper, envelopes, toothpaste, floss, conditioner, a hair brush, coffee, cocoa, chapstick, lotion! I feel like a human being again! I also got a few packs of Ramen noodles, which are a staple around here. I never thought Ramen could taste SO GOOD! Also, a couple bags of microwave popcorn. You smell popcorn all night in the Pod!

There is a microwave and hot water dispenser in the common area. There are also two tv monitors, one at either end, but the volume is never turned up so you must read the dialog box at the bottom of the screen. They are rarely on, but when they are, it's usually on TBS and there is usually some really stupid movie on.

We did get Animal Planet the other day and got to see a dog show and Pet Star. That was certainly a highlight of my weekend! But, it did make me heartsick for my doggies. My babies! I love dogs! They are the best. Better than humans for sure! Well, I've started on my outline for a book about this whole experience. Now that I've got a pencil and paper I can get started!

There are certainly lots of characters and stories in here. Some tragic. Some funny. Also the fact that this is a predominantly White county...and the whole Meth issue. The inner workings of a jail...would possibly be of interest to outsiders. We'll see.

Maybe someone will make a move out of! Haha "30-days in J-Pod"
Tell my Aunties who helped with my lawyer fee that I'm writing a book. They are Investors in it!
As to be expected, I am very anxious to get out of here and get back to my home, animals, work, etc. I am giving it until the first week of February for the bond hearing. I hope it can happen sooner, but that is how I'm pacing myself. I think we can hold out until then without resorting to contingency plans.

I'm anxious to get things going with the rental property. Have you given any thought to a home equity loan on it? That would give us money to pay back what has been borrowed and to finish the repairs to get it ready to sell. It can get repaid when it sells. I was thinking approximately $30k. It's a good solution. Nothing to be afraid of Sis. People do it all the time. You and Mom talk it over.

My stomach is no better, yet no worse. I am trying to eat the best I can in here, but it is very difficult to do. While you do get vegetables regularly, I have to say it's the worst tasting corn I have ever had. How does corn taste bad? Peas are good. Carrots ok. But when they serve rice, I am happiest.

Usually cereal or oatmeal in the a.m. with a little carton of milk or apple juice (sugar again). Bologna with cheese slice sandwich for lunch or peanut butter. Sometimes a chicken salad type thing that's "ok."

Meals for dinner are usually in a gravy over noodles or a soy type of thing that tastes like Salisbury Steak or chicken. These are ok. I'm ok with soy.

Any way, I thought you'd like to know what I was eating, Mom. Or not eating! Haha

Every now and then we get an Orange! Or an Apple! Maybe once a week. These are great days! It makes me think about what you told us about your Christmases as a child and getting an Orange or Apple was a special holiday treat! I get it now! They are a delicacy!

Yesterday, a mean, younger guard with a chip on her shoulder sent back our bananas...because of the chance someone would do something with one...smuggle it into their room and use it as a dildo! Can you believe it! I was really upset. I would love to have had a banana (to eat!) haha Oh well. No banana for you!

When I get out of here, I'm going to have a big salad with ranch dressing. Lots of fruit! A steak and baked potato! Let's make a date! Long Horn I'm trying to exercise and stay in shape. I'm doing stretches and we walk around in circles. Talk about a literal metaphor! We walk around the common area at night...doing laps. I am up to thirty sit ups, which is good for me. And I'm working on different types of moves, exercises, etc. and wrote out a routine.

I can't tell how much weight I've lost, but I know I've lost some. The other gal, Diana, had a chance to get on a scale when she went to Medical and had lost somewhere in the neighborhood of 10-13 pounds. She had more to lose than me as she is built like you, Mom, but I'm thinking I've probably lost about the same amount. At least 10 pounds I'm hoping! I do feel skinnier. The silver lining for all this. Weight loss! But what a way to have to do it!
With the small portions I'm eating and the exercise, it makes sense. Too bad they don't offer vitamins or anything healthy from the jail store. It figures!

I'm still hanging in there. I hope you are too. I feel better today and am more optimistic than I was on Friday after that ordeal in court...getting taken to a holding cell at 4:00 a.m., sitting there alone, cold on the concrete bench for three and a half hours until breakfast served at 7:30 a.m., sitting some more on the cold concrete bench for another hour. Then, taken to the courthouse in handcuffs. Sit in another cell for a few more hours. Sit in court and listen to them make all these accusations...The State of Georgia vs. Tess Sanderson...scary proposition.

Go sit in a cell again for another hour or two. Finally get taken back to the Detention Center. Sit in a holding cell again! Then, at last, get back "home" to the Pod.

Going to court is not so great, unless you get a good verdict. Hopefully, next time!

Love, Tess

February 1st,

Dear Brave Strong Daughter,

If you were Native American, I would name you Strong Beauty. It makes me feel proud that you accept this adversity and don't whine over it all...or is it pure anger? Any way, we'll get through all this and make the year a better or best year! It may have started off in a terrible way but we'll celebrate 2008 with success!

Isn't it a wonder how life can smack you over the head...geez...it's terrible. But at least we are all here to fight back.

I had a hard time reading your ordeal and what an insult to just assume you're guilty and arrest you like a common thief. Drat! All you can do is accept it until "they" let you go and you can get back to your life (which they have caused to fall apart). Once you get out you'll be able to save some parts of it. I hope it's not too late!

It's a mystery that the authorities have such power. What happened to the legal system? All I can figure is they deal with such awful people all day that when a nice one turns up they just treat them all the same, regardless. They are taught to be serious, somber and to work in any authoritative manner. It's dangerous work as some people do shoot at them. I am not eager to come to Atlanta although I will love to see you my Dear. I'm eager to get with Nardelli to list the investment house and get it sold. I can't do another payment. Aunt P is coming to help. I hope she doesn't get too riled up. Us two old ladies will do our best, but that place is I'm sure a big mess and needs to be cleaned out.

It is so very difficult for you I know. Such a loss. Such a waste. But try to remember you are smart, you are strong and you'll start over with more success and knowledge. Many others have had reason to start again, so try to take it easy and don't dwell on the sadness. Plan slowly, one day at a time. You'll make it!

Maybe when it's all calm and steady we can go to the ocean and rest somewhere. Just laugh and eat! Sounds good to me! I know Sis will like that too! I wonder if we'll ever get out of debt? Oh well, let's be proactive and look to the future. Once the present is cleared up…like bail and dismissal of charges. Once you're cleared then you can start but it seems the authorities keep tabs for years and years. I wonder if it will ever go away?

Your Aunt J sent $50. It's at the farm. Frank and Deb can get it to you If you need it. She sends her love!
Now that it's the 1st, I can send you some too. $20 money order is enclosed. I do what I can. Wish it could be more.

Love you,
Mom

Dear Love,

I am writing this letter to tell you not *how much* I love you, because that is beyond measure, but *how* I love you. You have been with me for over four years now and I believe you understand and know me.

I love you with open arms. I will never make you stay, but I will always hold you tight.

I love you with an open heart. I might not always tell you what you want to hear, but what I tell you will always be the truth and you will always know where you stand with me.

I love you with an open mind. I don't promise to agree with every decision you make, but I do promise to respect and support you in all your endeavors.

If you are looking for a man who can't live without you, I am not that man. If you are looking for a man who never wants to be without you, not even for a minute, I am he.

Your beauty and intelligence are a double-edged sword, especially to men. I understand this, maybe even deeper than you, because I am a man. Intelligence can be intimidating because most people are unsure of themselves, at least to some degree, and that is magnified when they are around someone like you who is confident and poised.

And of the beauty and sexuality you possess, that is in a league of its own. It has the power to make even the strongest man lose all reason, logic and pride and follow you around like a puppy.

I do not resent that power, I embrace it. To me you are the Warrior Queen and the double-edge sword you wield is my ally. You have never used your beauty to weaken or control me but instead it has always given me strength, inspiration and passion. Yes, I love to look at you. I always have from the first time I laid eyes on you. Always and often. All of you. All the time. I could write pages about how your beauty captivates me and maybe one day I will.

I love you as my friend. My best friend. Who do I trust more than you? Who do I share my innermost thoughts with more than you? In the best of times there is no one I would rather share excitement, joy, and good fortune with than you. In the worst of times there are few who I consider worthy to stand with me, much less walk with me. But I tell you it is an honor for me to walk with you through the storm.

I have seen grown men come apart in situations even less that what you and I have faced together. Then I've seen you come through troubles that were not of your own making and find good things, growth and learning in a situation that most would find only fear, anger and resentment in.

You stand strong. You walk with purpose. You walk with grace. You have my greatest respect. I don't give that to you, you have earned it.

I love you as my partner. How much you add to my life. Your insight and suggestions give me that extra edge in all my projects.

So many times you have turned my good writing into great writing. My weaknesses are your strengths and this is true in most every aspect of our relationship. I am also able to bounce ideas off you and get great creative input. Also, I love being part of your work and projects.

Partnership with you is in everything. Sometimes I lead, sometimes I follow, sometimes we make decisions together, but always we work together in harmony. In my experience it has been very rare to see any two people flow together like we do. We can do anything together.

Not only can we do anything together, we get to enjoy everything together. Everything is so much better sharing it with you. A great example of this is the farm. To me, it is the most beautiful place to live in the world! There is no place I would rather live. With that said, I have to tell you that the beauty of it is there for me because it is with you. Without you I would not even want to try it.

I also love you as my lover. I breathe with you because there is no where I had rather be and nothing I want to hide when I am alone with you. Everything about you thrills and excites me. I don't close my eyes because even in my greatest imagination does not compare to you and I don't want to stop looking. The way you feel, the way you smell, I can't seem to get enough. But when I am finally spent I am still there with my partner, my best friend, my soulmate.

Yours always,
Evan

Dear Mom,
I hope things are moving along for you there. Things are pretty much the same here...haha! (funny, but not so funny)

I have been frustrated lately because of a few things...first, the phones here were reset and I have not been able to call you or Sis...any long distance numbers. Hopefully it will get fixed and you will hear from me. Second, the other girlfriend included in this mess, Diana, got out on a bond yesterday...she didn't even have to go to court. Her attorney "walked it through" and got sign offs from the District Attorney and judge, while my bond hearing was moved due to the ice storm to Tuesday which gave me five more days in here. (sigh)

This is very frustrating, but I am trying to make the best of it and looking forward to Tuesday! Maybe I'll be able to see you and Aunt P then?

No other news other than I burned my tongue on my coffee this morning after heating it up in the microwave. Ouch! I drank some milk to try to make it feel better.

My roommate Chrissie is very nice and has a lot of stories to tell about her life so far at the ripe old age of 25 and keeps it interesting. We both think we are lucky to have ended up as roommates. She is a real sweetheart.

Another gal who is a friend in here, was Diana's roommate, fell out of the top bunk while sleeping the other night. She was rather frail any way and we think she broke her wrist and maybe some ribs.

It is a shame, but I think she'll be ok. She is a very sweet Indian (Native American) woman and one of my future clients with 5 acres to sell and she wants something out of this county when she sells...for good reason.

I guess that is all for now. I love you and Buster-Boy. Can wait to see you! Love to Sister too!
I'm hanging in there,
Tess

Dear Tess,
I know that there has to be an end to all this trouble some time. The sooner, the better to get you cleared and freed. I can't understand why they are keeping you and no bail? Seems so illegal to keep you for so long. How can you do your work and take care of the animals and all? I guess you are very worried about the horses, but from what I hear, they are doing ok but need worming. Once the darned 1st of the month comes around, I may be able to send some money to the vet. Sis has talked to DeeDee and seems all is well so far.

Don't know what's going to happen. May be come this weekend? I feel so old and incapable to help much. So much to think of...all money. I've run out of relatives to ask even though everyone has helped and I am grateful. I guess they love you cutie pie!
You rest, stay calm, keep Sis informed and stay healthy. Once you get out you'll need to work extra hard to catch up. Phew! You'll be busy.
Love you,
BIG HUG! Mom

Dear Love,

It is so good to get letters from you. I can't tell you in words how much you are in my heart. Of all the gifts I have been given in this life, it is the gift of you that fills my heart the most.

Hopefully my phone card will have come before you get this letter and hopefully very soon I will be home with you. I should have a court date this week and we can get a plan for the rental house. We should be able to pull out $30-$40k after paying back any loans. We will get your family paid back first and hopefully there will be a little left for us.

I am feeling the best physically I have in over 20 years. You are going to love it! I am so ready to get out and get started. No more drain people, no more loosing orendi, no more looking over my shoulder or feeling a need to hide anything. Freedom in every sense of the word.

It is very different for me, but I am over helping everybody. Yes I have been generous to a fault. So where are those people I have helped when I need help? Good riddance I say. What a relief. That should be worth and extra $50k-$100k a year just having the energy to work efficiently again. (that is my rant for the day).

Here is a Cherokee tale from my roommate:

TWO WOLVES

One evening an old Cherokee told his grandson about a battle that goes on inside people.

He said, "My son, the battle is between two wolves inside us all."

"One is evil. It is anger, envy, jealousy, sorrow, regret, greed, arrogance, self pity, guilt, resentment, lies, false pride, superiority and ego."

"The other is good. It is joy, peace, love, hope, serenity, humility, kindness, empathy, generosity, truth, compassion, and faith."

The grandson thought about it for a moment then asked, "Which wolf wins."

The grandfather replied, "The one you feed."

How well said.
My love always,
Evan

Dear Tess, my Sweet Girl!
Received your letters. You surely do write well and interesting. It's sad to see the envelopes stamped in red, "This letter was mailed from the Cherokee County Jail." So sad. You shouldn't be there. What a bunch of mistruth in all this. You're just a bystander and because of the slowness of the system, you're going to lose so much.

Don't they know that you are the bread winner so to speak. It's all your hard work and savings that you put into the farm and animals. So sad. Maybe you'll get out in time to help save it all. Maybe not.

I hope you realize that we are all working FOR YOU...trying to do what's best for the animals and the salvation of your property. It's just taking so long for the judicial system to work. We'll do the best we can.

I know you are a strong person and can take it. (Not like it, but withstand the hurt). I'll help all I can. I wonder if you'd come here to stay a while and rest up and regroup? Think it over. I know you'll need to stay in Atlanta area. I guess you're about nuts with worry. Try to stay calm and take it easy. Nothing you can do but keep us informed as to your wants and plans.

Difficult to make any plans while you're there, isn't it? I wish I had some good news. Well, I have no news, so that's good! We went to the dog park and Buster picked up every flea there and scratched all night. I put tree tea on him and that seems to help. Used the flea stuff you recommended and I don't know, maybe the bites remain. He scratched so hard that he fell off the couch!

So, try to be stronger than you already are. Let go. Let God. As they say. When you meditate, the world seems to come into focus and gets easier. It's a terrible thing that's happened to you and believe me, everyone in the family and friends are on your side. I know you are lonesome and scared and cold and hungry and should not be treated like this. Very hard to not get too angry.

I wish I could trade places, although you'd have to walk Buster four times a day, watch Guiding Light and take a lot of heart medicine. Oh yes, go to the bathroom every time you move! Haha So you don't need to want to trade spaces with me!

Well Kid, hang on and slowly the system will get around to helping you out. Drat! If only we had a lot of do-re-me...

We shall rise again! Or is it overcome?
The time is getting nearer to freedom!
Oxoxo,
Mom

PS - Just got your call - Sunday a.m.
Here I am supposed to be boosting your spirits and you're the one who makes me feel better. My goodness it's so mixed up, but you did make me feel better and less afraid and more hopeful. Thanks for being so smart. I like reading your account of the Cherokee County Detention Center, but it's hard to be objective when I know it's you in there. I feel sorry that this system has taken so many people hostage. I guess they are desperate to stop crime, even if it means arresting everyone.

It's scary to me because I lived through the take over of Germany (1940) that started slowing and quietly. Really frightening. People forget it's still America. I hope it'll change...for the better.

Burr...it's 19 degrees this a.m. Even Buster ran out and ran right back in. So chilly, but so invigorating. Reminds me of up North. Hope you're warm. I have on a t-shirt and my sweats. They are warm. It's the wind that's hard.

I had $3 so I bought two logs. Sis had brought 5 logs so I can stay cozy for another two days. It's cold in this place, especially the floor. I doubt there is any insulation. In the Summer it's ok.

Keep on writing. How's it at night? When you awake? Bathing, eating, what are the guards like? I like the evangelists. That was fun to read.

Love you,
Mom

February 1st,

Hi Mom!
Got your letters yesterday! Thanks for sending them! I really enjoy reading them and they are so encouraging.

I am hanging in as best I can. My stomach is hurting more than it has ever since I've been here, but it is because I was so stressed out last night due to my bond hearing today and dreading being taken out at 3:00 or 4:00 in the morning to sit in a freezing holding cell until 8:30 and then be driven over in handcuffs in a van to the courthouse.

Going to court...although good...is a very miserable experience. The cold being the worst of it and being alone...if you are...the second.
I worried myself sick due to the sleet and ice this morning and my hearing was moved to next Tuesday. Ugh

Evan's friend who got a bond, has to go through "pre-trial" and it's like probation where you have strict stipulations, must check in weekly by phone and monthly in person. He cannot have any contact with his girlfriend or any one else involved. I wonder if mine will be the same?

You asked about the food here, showers, if I'm cold, etc. Yes, I'm cold! I bought some thermals from the store and also have two pair of socks now and a t-shirt! I did get a pair of underwear (finally) and ordered another the week before, so I now have two pair of underwear! Hallelujah!

Our room is probably one of the warmest, being upstairs. We are guessing it's about 66-68 degrees. It's stark and chilly mostly, but if you move around, drink hot water or coffee, cuddle up in your blanket...double up the cotton throw and use your canvas pad cover like a sleeping bag or an additional cover on top, it's somewhat bearable. If I didn't have my socks and thermals, I'd be very cold.

The showers have warm water and I'm thankful for that. They aren't steamy hot, but that's ok. I'll take luke warm over cold any day! You push a button and it sprays for about 10 seconds and then you have to keep pushing it over and over. Like in a campground or something. They are at least private showers, not group, which is good.

As I've mentioned before, the food. Not much else to talk about. Sorry to be redundant. It's palatable at best. Barely. But when you're hungry, you eat what you get. As a Depression Baby, you know what it's like to be hungry, I know. They have a set schedule / menu of what you get each day, each week. We did get a small portion of cabbage the other day that made me think of you! I gobbled it up. It was the first time we had anything leafy or close to it since I've been here.

I try to be selective on what I eat. The stuff from the store makes up the difference, but still no fresh veggies. You can get tortillas from the store and a microwave rice type thing and make burritos, which are pretty good. I'm learning from the other gals the art of microwave jail cooking! They even made a cake for a woman here on her birthday out of something, I'm not sure what... a candy bar and twinkie mixed up together? They are very innovative when it comes down to it!

We don't get napkins or paper towels. Now THAT has been a MAJOR adjustment!

There is always Kool-aid made, but it's too sweet and causes urinary trat infections, so I stay away from that. If/when I do drink it, I dilute it a lot. I think it's the same mixture as the jello. I try and drink water as much as possible. There is a soda fountain dispenser on the drink station with a water button. I like to think the water is filtered somehow. It doesn't taste bad, so I'm hoping I'm right. But, I don't want to ask about it and burst my bubble!

I've had four roommates so far. The first two Staci and Sissy, the two sweet black women. Staci is still here. Sissy is out and I guess back at KFC/Taco Bell. The other two were young girls in here for dumb stuff...under age drinking, probation violation...testing positive for something when checking in or whatever. They were sweet, but young and dumb. Like I can talk, right? I'm not young, but I guess I'm dumb too! Haha

I hope I encouraged them a little with all my advice. Passing it on from you Mom! Maybe even talked them into getting into Real Estate. I think if I was 20 years old today, it would be really hard to be a wild one. Times sure have changed in the last 15-20 years.

My latest roommate, Chrissie, has two young children, is a very hard worker, and is in here for driving on a suspended license...while she was trying to get to work! She was very upset due to the circumstances that brought her here...a roommate not paying the rent with the money she gave them, getting evicted and then brought in when the evicting sheriff puller her up on the computer and the ticket showed up. They would not even let her get any of her kids pictures, birth certificates or anything and took her in, leaving all her things on the street. Wow! Unbelievable. So uncompassionate. Servants of the people.

I used to think our police officers were compassionate and respectful, but unfortunately not all are as they should be...at least not in this county...the younger ones in particular. Very snotty. And the female officers here, treat everyone in the Pod like little children. They are condenscending and disrespectful. I remember what you said about small minds in positions of authority. It's a scary proposition. Don't get me wrong...they don't "do" anything to you in here...it's just the petty things...verbal mostly...the banana incident.

What that officer did to poor Chrissie...over a traffic citation...I think was inexcusable as a human being. She didn't have much as it was, and now has nothing left. Her kids were with her mom in South Georgia thankfully, where she is from, and she does have the remainder of her possessions there at least. But, like I said, she was working really hard as a waitress, trying to get established with her husband up here. I hardworking young couple, trying to make it. But with a few set backs along the way, and then one fail swoop, got it all pulled out from under them, thanks to the roommate.

I guess a big lesson here and something I'm hearing over and over again...is that it's usually an association with another person that leads to your demise or legal problems, whether it's a roommate, boyfriend, friend or whoever...big lesson for me for sure!

Chrissie is from Okie Phenokie Swamp land near the Georgia Florida border. She's a red head with a long ponytail and freckles. A very pretty girl and very nice. She's not bass and dumb-dull like most of the others. We are talking about a few ideas for patents. Her dad is a welder and "gave away" a patent to Caterpiller, a part of mechanism that made the equipment stronger somehow and they even named it after him...Byrd-T or something like that. But he just gave it away over a steak dinner she said. Sounds like something Grandy Bill would do!

Any way, Chrissie had horses before and we talk about that, among other things.
She's had turtle soup before and gator bites too! Haha She reminds me of the character from Toy Story, cowgirl Jessie.

Chrissie is working on getting a bond so she can get back home down south and get busy re-establishing herself down there, having had enough of Cherokee County, which is a constant refrain here along with "never coming back again." We'll see about that in my case.

So I wait now for Tuesday. I'll have the money order from Aunt Joey sent here, just in case. I'm ok with Ramen, rice and tortillas until then. I am so hoping to be home next week and able to get back to work myself!

I love you Mom. I am doing ok. It will be ok...eventually. You just take care of yourself. If anything happened to you while I was in here or because I was in here, it would kill me. I am so sorry to have put you through all this. An old lady like you shouldn't have to deal with this type of worry. I am so sorry.

Tell Sis, Aunties and Cousins, I send my love and gratitude. I am trying to stay optimistic and all that. Hopefully this will all be over soon.

Love, Tess

Dear Love,
It is hard not to be able to hear your voice. Again so many things we take for granted and don't even realize we have until we no longer have them for a while. I will call every day and leave you a message on the greeting and at least let you know I'm ok. I will call my Mom and sister every two or three days as well so leave any messages you want to with them.

I am so ready to come home.

I will be out soon. I feel it now. I have things to do out there for both for us and things I'm called to do. I believe I have learned the secret of those I should help and those I should stay away from. It is a very subtle thing, but I am practicing how to recognize it and I have so much opportunity in here on a daily basis that I am honing it to a very sharp edge. Rather than think about it, I have to close off my thoughts and look to "see" with my inner knowing and truly be unattached to the outcome.

I will be able to make the changes we need to make at the farm with the situations you are having to deal with now. It will be win win. I have seen that also. It is time to scale down and build a solid foundation. We will have the help we need and we will have time and energy to do the rest ourselves.

If I use my money or our resources to keep people from learning their lessons...one of my previous bad habits. I would not be allowed to be successful if I keep doing that.

No more leeches. If you ever suspect me of doing that or thinking about doing that, call me on it. Ask me to step back unattached and look to see. This is very important. I would like to believe I will always do this, but just in case, there is a tool for you.

The success I have seen for us is unlimited, except what limitations we put on ourselves. Remember this part of our growth can be together if we walk together. It is still each our own choice where we go and what we do but we can choose to learn many things together at this stage.

As far as my spiritual path is concerned, I am working toward devoting 10% of my time learning and 10% of my time teaching. I am not sure what this is going to require, but I will work on it until I get the right balance. Also, as I have said, I am going to structure my workload to a 40-50 hour week so there will be time for us and time for the farm.

Efficiency is the key there...time management as you always said. I am learning too. The first thing I am going to do when I come home (after I spend some incredible time with you) is organize my part of our room and office.

I hope you and all of the dogs, cats and horses are doing well. I miss you and hope to see you soon.

Love always,
Evan

Dear Love,
Don't worry about the truck and tools. They are only things. The greatest gifts we have are each other, out family, our true friends and our animals. All the rest of it can be replaced or even let go of.

Did I tell you today I love you? Of course I did, many, many times. Even if you are not where my voice can reach you, I am still saying it, still feeling it. We are solid. The world around us might go through a few changes now and then, but that just gives us chances to grow.

Have you noticed that wherever we are and whatever situation we find ourselves in, we both make friends and find positive things and growth in what would appear to be a negative situation? I am proud of you and I am honored to be with you. I want you to know that you inspire to be my very best.

I am very excited about our future. Remember my prayers were answered in one amazing instant. I am preparing myself for the next phase of our adventure together…just like I prepared myself when I knew you were on your way into my life. The time in here is not being wasted.

Be strong and be you!

Love always,
Evan

Dear Love,
I cannot tell you how good it was to hear you voice. I really did not know that it would make that much of a difference, but it did. It's like something changed inside of me.

Once again, it's late at night and all it quiet. I know nothing has changed physically about my situation but I have such inner peace.

What Joe M said made a difference too. In my heart, I have no ill feelings of any kind toward him, not that there were ever any bad feelings, just a lot of tension and I never really realized was there.

There is a proverb in the Bible I have always loved. Proverbs 16:7 When a man's ways are pleasing to the Lord, he makes even his enemies be at peace with him. I used to think about that a lot when I was in my 20s and early 30s. I came to the conclusion that I was my only enemy. If any human being had animosity toward me, it had to be because of something I had done wrong either to them or even something unrelated somewhere else in my life.

I want to address the disconnection you sometimes feel. I have needed to go deep inside myself and really look at many things. My hectic life before now never allowed me to do that. It has taken all this time up to now just to get where I am now…at peace with myself. No one is pulling on me any more and I am like you with being over anyone using me or taking advantage of my generosity and resources.

I am not blocked with you any more at all. If you are ready to share everything, I am ready to share everything. Hopefully that time will come soon.

I want you to know that my new self is a man you will be proud to be with and a man who is honored to be with you. I'm really not anything new. I have just shed those things that have weighed me down physically, mentally and spiritually. I have also worked on exercising and toning up those last three things as well.

I want to share another favorite Proverb with you…Proverbs 16:3 Commit to the Lord whatever you do and your plans will succeed.

The Native American teaching of this is: Be in alignment with the Great Spirit.

I thought about this as I was writing this letter and it came to me that I had put God first in asking for you. I let go of everything and thanked the Universe for all that I had been given in past relationships and was truly ok in my heart if I could never have it all in one person…The One. I was ok being alone. I asked for everything I knew I wanted (in a person) and anything else I needed but didn't know to ask for.

Asking for what God thought I would need is truly one of the best things I have ever done.

After all this time together, it is even more obvious how special and sacred our relationship is.

I know sometimes you feel like the lone wolf, but you are not alone. You are the alpha female wolf and I am the alpha male wolf. We are still each a wolf and can survive on our own under most any circumstance and environment. Remember also in the pack, only the alphas breed and mate for life.

Things are changing for the better and I will be out as soon as the Universe if ready for me to leave. Soon, I hope. I have learned much and I have been given opportunities to lead and teach as well. I am thankful to be able to give back because so much has been given to me.

My sister said to me, "Don't get too comfortable in there because we need you out here." Believe me, it is not comfortable in here, but I am at peace and it seems that as each day goes on I learn more and more.

If you hear from Barbara, tell her I am very sorry things turned out this way. I know she and her husband must be furious about finding out what was done in their house and I can understand if that ruins our friendship. Tell her also the Brian and Diana were just there to help clean the upstairs and outside to get the house in good condition before it was vacated. I hope she will let them get their things out of there because, just like her, they had nothing to do with what was downstairs.

How are the dogs? How are the horses?

The card with the horses is beautiful and you are my dream woman. All the letters have really made a difference and have given me strength and many times filled my heart.

I love you and I will be with you soon.
Evan

Dear Love,
I know I've often said that life with you is like a surround sound home theater compared to life without you being a small black and white TV. I realized today that the truth is I have never actually thought of having to live life without you until today. I can tell you that the complete and utter emptiness is nothing like any black and white TV I've ever seen. I lost it for a moment.

I never really understood how integrated you are in everything…every aspect of my life. You fill my heart and make everything I set out to do not only possibly but also enjoyable and with purpose.

I have blamed you for my unwillingness to be close to you, but it is not you. It has been me. I have kept things from you to keep from having arguments and it has hurt our relationship. I am ready to share everything and not hold back any more. Together we can do anything and I mean anything. I have never "seen" anything like it.

I truly believe you know this now but I want to say it again…my heart belong to you and you alone. I love and care for everyone else as I always have, but make no mistake my heart belongs to only you. I cannot imagine spending this life with anyone else.

We have had good times, great times, hard times and bad times and we are still together. During the hard times and bad times we have always been a team and worked together and came through everything we've been up against. It is very different to be away from you, even for one day. Know that I am always with you…even when we are apart. When the good times are here, believe me there is no one I had rather share them with than you. I can't even sit on the opposite side of the table from you when we are together! You would be too far away!

I want to share a prayer with you that I said one night before all this happened. I asked for help with all of those people and situations that were draining me. I didn't know what to do to change it. I asked for help with my spiritual path to be able to walk closer to God as I once had. I asked to be free from looking over my shoulder and be able to be proud of the things I do for a living and to be able to be a good example for my son. Also to be a good son to my mother and son in law to your mother…one they could both be proud of and one that could be open and honest about everything he did. And finally, I asked for the blocks in our relationship to be lifted and for us to be able to share the gift we have been given of each other and the closeness we can have.

It is very easy to see how the current situation can be a major part of answering all of those requests. Believe me, it is not the way I would have chosen but I can certainly see how quick and efficient the method is.

I want you to know that we can do anything together. I believe in everything you are doing with the web site and your real estate career. When I get out I am ready to hit the ground running and do my part to strengthen our relationship, our finances, our home and our family. I really am crazy about you!

I want you to know and never doubt my feelings for you. We are solid. I have never changed since Blue Ridge. Even before that I knew you were coming and I got ready for you. I didn't quite have all the loose ends tied when you arrived (I still have a few…taxes, ticket, Tacori), but I did have most of it ready. At any rate, I changed everything in my life to flow in the direction of being with you. I have never regretted in any way doing that and I have never looked back.

I know I tell you often that my worst day with you is better than my best day with anyone else. Don't you know that on my worst day with you, I still have you! That I would never trade for any 10 others or even all of the material wealth in the world.

I wrote this letter over several days and it reflects the different moods I was in at the time. The last few parts were written after I got the pictures of the farm and the horses and since then I have felt like I am on top of the world! It is ironic because even though I am caged, I feel free. The things that weighed so heavy on me…the things I prayed for help with are lifted. I don't know how long I will be here but I am sure it will be the length of time the Universe needs for me to be here.

I love you, I miss you,
Evan

Dear Love,
I love you and I miss you. I'm hanging in there. Before I forget, have you cancelled the truck insurance? If you have not, make sure you do so that don't suspend anyone's license.

I guess I haven't said much about my life in here, so I'll fill you in.

We've won the movie cart and the 2-liter Coca-Colas last week and this week. I believe J-Pod got 2nd place a few times and got the other movie cart. Our average score is 95 or 96 including the inspections from the corporals outside.

When I first arrived, it wasn't like that at all. One of my roommates is an older fellow named Jim Jones and his is from Ball Ground. He pretty much single-handedly started the trend of all of us taking pride in our room and it spread through the Pod.

A deputy named Whitley brought in four Moon Pies and said the cleanest room gets them. Of course our room won them so we were saying this is how we do it in Ball Ground. We won 5 out of 7 times that he did that, with only one other room taking the other 2 times.

It's not really a big thing, but in jail there is not a lot you can do to take pride in yourself. On our next outside inspection, the female corporal stopped at our cut and said, "You guys have a really clean room." Our pod got an 81 up from 60s and 70s scores we had been getting. I thought, "Wow, did our room really stand our enough to make her stop and take notice?" The corporals usually never say a word to any of us during an outside inspection.

The next outside inspection a week or two later, I went to all the other rooms and made sure they were as neat and clean as ours, even if I had to roll up the towels and arrange the shelves myself, which I did on several rooms. The pod got a 93, with perfect 10s in 6 out of 10 categories. It was amazing to hear so many of the inmates at dinner saying how we all came together and "threw down" to get such a good score.

Our next outside inspection got a 96 and we averaged 95+ on our dailys and we got 1st place...the movie cart and 2-liter Coca-Cola for each room. It is now a tradition that Romeo Pos is the cleanest and most disciplined Pod in the jail. The guards now expect the best from us. They look for that in R-Pod and they find it. Remember what you look for is what you find.

I know these are small things, but it has shown me that even in a Pod of 64 inmates, one or two men can make a difference. The vibe in here is one of pride and there are always more than enough volunteers for all of the clean up duties...which used to be assigned by room. And, most of those are the people who used to be troublemakers wit the "don't care" and "F-you" attitude...the toughest, meanest guys in here...you know...the guys that hang out with me during free time.

I have been working on my physical and spiritual self. I workout. I fast every other week for two days. I read the bible and I study Proverbs every day. I use and teach the Native American teaching. I live, walk and breathe that no matter what others around me do. I still have to be me. Yes, there are ups and downs, good days and bad days, but I am growing stronger and stronger.

I have learned from everyone in here. I have seen my spirit change many in here. I have seen many amazing "coincidences" that could only be orchestrated by a power much greater than us. I have spoken face-to-face with everyone in here who has been charged with me. Some were put in my Pod deliberately to get information from me and others I have been able to see by means that I can't reveal at this time.

By the way, do not trust Troy with any information. Also do not say anything that could incriminate yourself or me to anyone. I do not think you know anything but if somehow you do, understand ears are everywhere. This goes for friends and family and real estate clients or cell tower scouts! Remember the phone are probably being listened to also. Enough said about that.

In this letter I am filling you in on my life in here…so back on the subject. I have had a haircut (just the back and an evening up of the top), and I have clipped my nails. I have everything I need for here. I've got a t-shirt, two pairs of socks, thermal shirt, plenty of money on my books, etc. etc. Yes, I have many friends…some who I will probably see on the outside later. Everyone gets along in our Pod and when new people come in, we help them get acclimated and tell them what we expect of them. The movie cart and Cokes each weekend don't hurt either.

I haven't had to want for anything in here. Most everyone shares and helps out. I've played some good chess in here also. I bought a second chess set for the Pod last month, so now more people are able to play.

I made a pact with my friend Tommy that we will hold each other accountable to cherish and treasure the women that God gave each one of us. Do you remember when we first got together and I told you I was always on my best behavior with you? I truly was for a long time and I began to let it slip. I do cherish and treasure you and I promise to give you my best. We might not always agree on everything, but I will always love, honor and respect you with my highest standards.

I miss everyone and all the animals. I know you have a tough decision to make about Lady. You might consider just leasing her or having a buy back claus (or keeping her). I know we could use the money, but I am doing my part to be able to make it without that if you don't really want to sell her. I am just thinking of other options. I know you will make the best decision. It's just hard for me to imagine the farm without her.

Let's see...what else I have been doing? I put together a marketing strategy for the car lot I'm planning to do when I get out. I will be able to do it with or without Steven, but I really hope it is with him. I've got some great ads and a unique mail out campaign that I am sure will be successful beyond anything that's ever been done in our area. It is of the same magnitude that I saw with your web site. Whoever I decide to go with will own our niche, lock stock and barrel. It has unlimited potential. I don't often see that in anything.

Anyway, it's very exciting. I will build it with a firm foundation and grow it at the rate it can support itself comfortably. Believe me. I have learned that lesson.

As for staffing, I will not carry anyone. They will make me stronger, or they will not be there one second longer than it takes me to fire them or not hire them in the first place. That lesson is well learned too...thank you Mick, Glenn, etc.

I have a fresh slate with almost everything now. Imagine all we can do together. I will balance home, work, play and pursuit of spiritual growth much better this time. Yes, I do have some debts to pay, although they are less that what those people claim. They are figured in the equation.

I have considered the car lot many times but have been too spread out and drained to take it on. If Steven and I can work together, that will be my only job and I will give it my all. Any other financial endeavor will be a hobby behind being home at a reasonable hour and all the other things I have mentioned.

I would rather work with Steven than anyone else out there in that field. He would be in a position to do what he likes to do best…buy cars. I would be in a position to run production, sales and marketing, which is what I like to do. I have put together bank financing, which he has never had and I have some of the best bodymen and sales people already committed to me as soon as I open the doors.

When you see my marketing strategy, you will know why I am so excited about it. I am chomping at the bit to get going, so hopefully I will be out of here soon.

By the way, the tractor is $10k. Stay focused on the big items and don't let something small like the washer and dryer I paid $200 for take your energy away from making real money.

I know you are back to think about real estate now and I know you will be successful. The next item up is the rental house. I've got a very good prospect at $165k. That will be the next large amount I will focus on bringing in. And congratulations on your recent test. I am very proud of you!!!

We will get through all of this. We will be even better than we were before. Any couple can make it in good times. We can make it in all times!

My love, passion, friendship and respect always,
Evan

Dear Love,
I hope everything is well. I miss you as always...every day and often.

This is late at night on my second day of fasting, so everything is starting to clear. It is very peaceful and quiet. There are so many things I want to share with you when we are together again, but tonight it will only be this letter.

There are things in here that are almost magical. People that you would never expect to get along at all, doing things for each other beyond what normal friendships on the outside would do.

My most recent roommate is a 33 year old black man. When he got here a week or so ago he had the typical attitude you would expect of anyone young and upset, put in this situation. Add in the fact that he had been high on cocaine when he came in and had lost his 39 year old brother the previous week and I'm sure that the word "upset" only touches the surface. He slept most of the first two days.

The first real conversation I had with him started off pretty rough. When he had gotten up and finally seemed coherent enough to talk I told him about how we all do our part to keep the Pod clean and about the movie cart, etc. His response was, "I don't give a F about the movie cart or anything else when I'm in jail." I said, "I know you don't right now, but others in this call and in this Pod do, so at least consider them."

He immediately said, "You know, you are right. It's my bad attitude and I've never thought of anyone other than myself in jail." What a different response than the first fight you would have expected to have.

From that moment forward he seemed to be a different person, and that's only the beginning of this story. A few days later his father took a turn for the worse and was not expected to live much more than a few days. At one point I saw my other roommate, Jim Jones, hugging him and telling him that we were all there for him. I told you about Jim leading the Pod to the tradition of excellence we now have in the last letter. What I didn't tell you was about Jimmy the man. I would describe him as true, old school southern no B.S. working man. He pours concrete for a living and would seem more likely to be at a KKK rally than showing such compassion to a young, muscular black man with tattoos.

It goes on from there. The fellow's father died the next day. Think about that…he's in jail, just got in jail, and could not go to his father in the hospital while he was sick or go to the funeral home when he died. Remember too, he had just lost his brother a little over a week ago, not to mention the problems you have when you are not able to work and make a living. Again, not the response you would expect.

He has handled his grief and circumstances with strength and heart that is an example for any man to aspire to. He also told us how much of a difference have had made in him and how his perception of things has changed since being here with us. This is not his first or even second or third time in this jail, not to mention others.

I have seen this so much in here. It's like everyone is ready to make changes for the better and it just takes a small push to make it all take action. I keep hearing from almost everyone that we are here for a reason, a blessing in disguise or something similar from 90% or more of the inmates in here. My Pod is a medium security with mostly felon charges and most of the guys are strong, tough, tattooed and no B.S. There is no weakness in here. There is also no stealing, cheating or disrespect. There is teamwork, co-operation and compassion.

I have been told many times that this is not typical, but as you know I had no idea what to expect and I always look for the best in people. What we look for, we find. It's only a matter of having others look for the same things. I believe that if your heart is right, it doesn't take much.

The way you have handled yourself in these circumstances makes me love you even more. You went to jail for something you had nothing to do with. Yet instead of being resentful and angry, you start writing a book and tell me it's all a blessing in disguise.

Instead of crumbling and falling apart, you gain strength and look for the good things that come out of all this. You gain character and a perspective that can only come from weathering adverse conditions.

How could I ever truly give my heart to anyone less? Where would I even look to find another like you? We have come through many storms together and we have loved each other with more power than all of them.

I loved you then.
I love you now.
Evan

Dear Love,
It is evening again and of course I would much rather be at home with you. I know I say things like this often, but I have to tell you I would rather be in here with you in my heart, than out there without you.

I hope you are doing well. It's about 10:45 pm so I guess you must be snuggled up with the dogs. Be sure to pet them for me and tell them I miss them. Tell you mom and Buster I miss them too. I hope she is enjoying her stay with you. I'll cook you both a nice dinner when I get home.

The weather is so beautiful outside these last few days. It makes me think of the farm, our home, every time I walk into the basketball court and feel the fresh air and sunshine. I think of it and am at peace and happy for the moment. Of course I miss everything but I can still feel it in me. I have been so fortunate to have experienced such beauty and to have shared it with the one in my heart…my lover, best friend, partner and soulmate.

I know I have never said soulmate to describe our relationship before, so let me tell you why I now feel this way.

Everything we've had together has always been wonderful and has had unlimited potential in all areas, and this has been true even on our bad days together.

These first few years we were learning from each other. This has been a good thing because each of our weaknesses has been in areas of the other's strengths. In these particular areas we often didn't understand each other but we were both able to make changes, learning from the other's strength.

I have learned much from you and many things have hit home since I've been in here (finances, drain people/losers, taking care of personal property, etc.)

Now I feel I understand you and am understood. Many of the letters you have written have said the same things I have written to you at the same time.

My mother has so often said that when she is talking to you she feels like she is talking to me because our thoughts and attitudes are so alike. I do feel understood and not alone. Sometimes lonely but never alone.

In my prayer I asked for our relationship to strengthen and be all that it could be. I would have never wished our current situation on us but I can so clearly see how much strength and understanding it has given both of us.

The next phase of our journey, much of our learning will be together, rather than from each other. I am not the same man who first came in here, not physically, mentally or spiritually. Look for the best. Expect the best. Accept no less.
My love always, even more today than ever before,
Evan

Dear Love,
I hope you are having a good day today. I know things are hard for you and I know all of the additional stress and negativity is not making things any easier. Be strong like we both know that you are.

I am sending you energy that you have asked for and also healing for the bleeding and for fertility.

Hopefully, I will be out soon and can help with the finances and workload. I can't wait to see you, feel you. It has been way too long.

I love and miss you much,
Evan

Dear Love,

I was just thinking about you like I so often do, so I decided to write. I still don't know anything new about my bond hearing, but the lawyer did say to try back Monday. In the meantime, it's Friday so it's another long weekend.

I think about kissing you a lot these days. It seems like way longer than the time it has been. I am opened up now and can't wait for you to take advantage of it. We will make up for lost time when we get back together and even more than that when we make new time.

I will take you to places we didn't even go to in Blue Ridge. I no longer have the chains that bound me then.

I have told you all these years that any time I have seen or talked to any one else it always makes me love and appreciate you even more. I've got a new dimension to add to that now. Today I was flipping through a music magazine and saw a picture of some new actress and her haircut and the shape of her eyes and lips reminded me so much of you, it made me miss you. I must be really crazy about you when anything I notice about anyone else makes me long for you.

It really is like that for me all of the time. When people talk about their wives, girlfriends, exes and such, it makes me appreciate you so much.

Whenever I think of anyone else in my past, it makes me love and appreciate you and all we have even more.

You know I always like to think of the good things about people as opposed to bad and even thinking of others best qualities, you always shine through and fill me with warmth.

I'm hanging in here. I hope to be out soon and get going with the next phase of my life. It looks very promising.

I will write you again soon.
I love you and miss you!
Evan

Dear Love,
I finally got a court date for the bond hearing.

I want you to know the first thing that came to my mind….I want to cook dinner for you. Isn't that crazy? I was thinking about what I would make for you and your Mom if she is there. It's funny what things seem to matter and mean the most to a person.

During the most romantic weekend of my life, what still stands out to me the most is the two of us cooking dinner together. I already knew that I would always be with you and when we were preparing the meal it just showed me so many things.

First of all, I was so excited to be there with you. It made me tingle inside. I guess it really didn't matter what we were doing…it was all great. I think about how we worked together and how we each brought different things to the meal. It is the first thing we did together and it is so symbolic of how we work so well and flow together and how wonderful the result always is. Also, it felt so right to be there with you.

I have never felt like that with anyone else in my entire life. I still feel that way.

We let some of the magic be covered up by all of the stressful things we have gotten ourselves into, but I can assure you it is ALL still there. I can feel it.

We have an opportunity to have even more than we had then, all we have to do is make it important to us. It is important to me. I have been getting ready. I've had three months of reflection, working out, letting go, learning, teaching, giving and receiving. I don't even look the same. I feel better than I have felt in over 20 years. Do you realize I've been given everything I asked for in my prayer…even somethings I needed but didn't know to ask for.

We have more than just a fresh start. We have each other and a beautiful farm and all of the growth we have achieved, and all the magic we had when we first got together. To keep the fire burning we have to both feed it, make it important every day. I am doing my part, even now. When I work out, I think of you. I do sets of 11 and 22 and now that I'm stronger I do sets of 33 on some things.

I always think of you and appreciate you when any other relationship is mentioned or thought of …just like I always have. I'm telling you, now we have more than we had and we have been through hard times and have made it. Let's always make whatever time we have together special. To do any less would not be honoring the one who had given us this gift.

I should be out next week. We will make everything happen. I'll see you soon!
Love always,

Evan

5/4

Dear Love,
I wish that I could say that everything will always be good with us, but as hard as we try there will be times when we upset each other. It crushes me inside when I've said things to upset you or hurt you in any way. I can't take back words already said, I'll have to live with that, but I can learn from the situation and not repeat the same mistake again.

It is hard for me to let go of control of thinks like the rental house because most of the time I think I'm the only one who can do anything right there.

Unfortunately, my past experience with most construction workers has only served to reinforce those feelings. I am sure anything you pick out will be beautiful and I should not worry about it. Your track record alone should show me that. The cabinets are absolutely wonderful and your choices and décor at the farm are great also. I will also say again, I have never loved a place any where near as much as I love the farm and you picked that out without any involvement from me whatsoever.

I am very committed to our relationship, just as I always have been and even now more so. We have come through so many hardships and trials. I am honored to have shared these last few years of my life with you.

My first focus when I get out is to finish the rental house. At least then it will become an asset and can be rented or sold and not be hanging over our heads. I have a little money available to me to do that with and I am also going to do some work to bring a few thousand a month toward our bills. My next focus will be to finish the last part of the farm. When I am done with those two things we will at least be in solid shape financially.

I do not want to ever lose you, but want you to know that if you want to leave me for any reason you can have it all. I have never in my life felt at home like I do with you and at our farm, but without you it would all be meaningless.

These last few weeks have been hard on me also and I too often feel numb. I am doing the things that I can do for us in here and am working on myself as well. I try to stay optimistic about everything as much as possible. Sometimes I have a bad day but for the most part I do ok.

I am committed to you and all of the things we are doing together. I know it is hard on you with me not being there physically, but just know I love you and should be back with you very soon. Pet all of the animals for me and tell them I miss them.
I love you always,
Evan

5/5

Hello Love,

I feel much better mow. It has been a really rough week and I guess I just felt out of touch. I have been here over four months now and it is wearing on me a little. Anyway, I am looking forward now and thinking about all of the things that we have.

I can't wait to be with you again. It will be better than it has ever been. In spite of all of the obvious negative things about being here, I feel that it has been a good trade. As much as I would like to believe that I would have gotten my act together, I really don't think I would have any time soon and certainly not to the point of where I am now. I really believe I have added many years to my life by make the changes I have been able to make, and certainly, the quality of my life is much better.

The exercise I am doing is really helping. I am up to sets of 40 push ups and 60 sit ups at a time for a total of 200 each. What a difference. I could only do 15 push ups and 20 sit ups when I first started. I can't wait for you to be with the new and improved version of me!

I also want to thank you for writing me. It really makes a difference when I get a letter from you. It still makes my heart sing when I hear from you. I miss you and all the animals and the farm, the beauty of everything. Hopefully I will be home soon. Love always, Evan

Isaiah 61:1

"The spirit of the Lord God is upon me,

because the Lord has anointed me;

He has sent me to bring good news to the oppressed,

to bind up the brokenhearted,

to proclaim liberty to the captives,

and release to the prisoners."

Made in the USA
Columbia, SC
13 November 2023